O9-AIE-708

Discount
Diva

Meghan
Murphy

KINGFISHER
a Houghton Mifflin Company imprint
222 Berkeley Street
Boston, Massachusetts 02116
www.houghtonmifflinbooks.com

First published in 2007
2 4 6 8 10 9 7 5 3 1

Text copyright © Cathy Hopkins 2007
Cover illustration copyright © Eliz Hüseyin 2007

The moral right of the author has been asserted.

All rights reserved under International and
Pan-American Copyright Conventions

LIBRARY OF CONGRESS CATALOGING–IN–PUBLICATION DATA
has been applied for.

ISBN 978-0-7534-6131-0

Printed in India
1TR/0507/THOM/SCHOY/60BNWP/C

Zodiac Girls

Discount Diva

Cathy Hopkins

KINGFISHER
BOSTON

Chapter One

The Crazy Maisies

I wish, I wish, I wish I could go, I thought when our teacher Miss Creighton first made the announcement.

". . . I will be taking names from all you eighth-grade girls in the next week," she continued. "All those who want to go must register before the end of May, which only gives you two weeks."

A school trip to Venice. Two weeks in sunny Italy. I wanted to go more than anything, ever, since the beginning of eternity and even before that.

"You going to put your name down, Tori?" asked Georgie when the bell rang and we headed out of the classroom for our lunch break.

I shrugged my shoulders as if I didn't really care. "Maybe," I said.

"I definitely am," said Megan, catching up with us and linking arms. "Mom said I could go on the next school trip, wherever it was."

"Me, too," said Hannah, linking arms with Megan.

"Me, too," said Georgie. "Which means *you have* to come, Tori. It wouldn't be the same without you. The

Crazy Maisies hit Europe."

Me, Hannah, Megan, and Georgie. We called ourselves the Crazy Maisies. My mom used to call me that when I was little and acting silly. Me and my friends act silly a lot, hence the name.

"Venice isn't *that* great," I said. "Too many tourists. Florence is much more interesting." Ha. Like I'd been to either of them. Not. But I had heard my well-traveled Aunt Phoebe saying that Venice was so full of tourists these days that you could hardly move.

"You *have* to come," said Hannah. "And so what if there are loads of tourists? We'll be four of them!"

"Yeah," said Georgie. "Italy, here we come!"

I felt a sinking feeling in my stomach. I was *so* going to miss out, but I could never tell them the real reason why I couldn't go.

"Si, signora, pasta, cappuccino, tiramisu," I said, trying to remember all the Italianish words that I had ever heard and to distract them from trying to persuade me to go. I'd have to think up some excuse that they'd all buy later.

"Linguine, Botticelli, spaghetti . . ." Megan joined in.

"Da Vinci, Madonna, pizzeria, Roma," said Hannah.

Then they started singing a song that we'd done in music class last quarter. We'd had a substitute teacher who had us singing songs from around the globe. "Trying to broaden your horizons," he said as he taught us folk songs from Italy to Iceland. By the end of the quarter, however, I think he was glad to broaden his horizons and move on to another school where the students weren't tone-deaf.

"When the moon hits your eye like a big pizza pie, that's *amore* . . ." my friends chorused off-key and in terrible Italian accents.

A few ninth-grade girls sloped past and looked at us as if we were crazy. I play-acted that I wasn't with them, but Georgie dragged me back, and Hannah and Megan got down on their knees, put their hands on their hearts, and continued hollering away at the tops of their voices.

Crazy. They all are. And they'll have a great time in Venice, that's for sure. Another thing that was for sure was that no way would I be going with them. Not a hope in heck.

During break, we went out into the playground, found a bench on the sunny side, and did each other's hair. When we first met, only Georgie, out of the four of us, had long hair. After a short time hanging out together, we all decided to grow our hair to the same length so that we could play hairdresser, and long hair is best for experimenting with. Georgie and Meg are blond, although Megan's hair is thicker and golden blond, while Georgie's is fine white-blond. Hannah and I have

7

ordinary brown hair, although Hannah has had chestnut highlights put in hers lately. It looks totally cool. I'd love to have highlights, but that's another thing to add to the "not going to happen unless Mom wins the lottery" list.

I think Georgie's the prettiest of the four of us, although Megan and Hannah are good-looking in their own ways too. Hannah could pass for being Mexican. She has olive skin and amazing dark brown eyes, which look enormous when she puts on makeup, and Megan has a sweet face, cornflower-blue eyes, and a tiny nose like a doll. Out of all of us, boys mostly pay attention to Georgie and me, though. Hannah and Megan say it's because I'm pretty too, but sometimes I wonder if the main reason that boys talk to me is to get in with Georgie.

I'm not huge in the confidence department. Some days I can look okay—I know I can—but I could look lots better if I got my hair done professionally and bought some fab new clothes and makeup, but I doubt if that's going to happen anytime soon. Reason being, my family is broke and a half, so it's hard trying to keep up on the appearance front. Most of my clothes come from secondhand stores, but I worry that my friends will find out. At school, girls who don't wear the latest designer clothes get called Discount Divas because their clothes don't have recognizable labels. Megan, Georgie, and Hannah have no idea that I'm Queen Discount Diva.

"I think we should go for a really sophisticated look when we're in Venice," said Megan as she pulled back Georgie's hair and began to braid it.

"No. I think we should wear it loose," said Hannah.

"Yeah," said Georgie. "Loose and romantic-looking. There might be some cute Italian boys to flirt with."

Oh, no! Boys! Italian boys. I hadn't thought of that. What if one of my friends got a boyfriend and I wasn't there to share it all with them? What if all *three* of them got boyfriends and had their first kiss? It might happen. I've heard that Italy is a really romantic place. *Romeo and Juliet* happened over there, and they were *way* loved up. I've also heard that Italian boys are very hot-blooded. (I'm not totally sure what that means and whether they really do have hotter blood than us on account of living in a warmer climate. Whatever.) Apparently they are more forward than American boys, who mostly seem more interested in computers than they do in girls. Anyway, I would be left so far behind in the game of love. I'd be like Cinderella left at home while everyone else went to the ball. Eek! That would be freaking *tragic*. The Crazy Maisies do everything new together—that way we can talk about it all and see how we all feel.

"Ow," said Hannah with a wince as I brushed her hair up into a ponytail. "You're hurting me."

"Sorry," I said and made myself brush more gently. I didn't mean to take my frustration out on her, but all the talk for the next few weeks would be about the trip. And then they'd go, and I'd be by myself. And then they'd come back, and all the talk would be about the trip again. And I'd have nothing to say because I wouldn't have been there. I'd be left out. It would be awful.

Luckily, Megan changed the subject and began making plans for the weekend. A new comedy was playing at the local movie theater. Of course, everyone was up for seeing it.

"Cool!" said Georgie. "And we could go for a snack afterward."

Megan and Hannah nodded enthusiastically. "Lots of those spicy, cheesy taco thingies. I loooove them."

"Ice cream for me," said Georgie. "Pistachio with . . . strawberry."

"Pecan fudge is my fave," I joined in.

"We'll have to do the early show, around six o'clock, or Mom won't be able to pick me up," said Hannah.

I did a quick calculation as they were discussing how they were going to get there and back and what they were going to eat. I'd need money for the movie. Snack. Coke. Nope. No way could I do it on my allowance money. I get around one fourth of what my friends get, and some weeks when things are really tight, Mom can't give us anything at all—us being me, my older sister, Andrea, and my two brothers, William and Daniel. I took a deep breath and got ready to apply my usual philosophy: when the going gets tough, the tough bluff it.

"I can't make it tonight. Mom got me and Dan and Will tickets for the Cyber Queens gig."

"The Cyber Queens? Wow! You *lucky* thing!" said Georgie.

"You've kept quiet about that this week," said Megan. "Those tickets are like the hottest in town."

Hannah playfully punched my arm. "Yeah. Why didn't you tell us?"

"Mom only told us last night. It was a surprise for when we got home."

"A surprise? That's *so* cool," said Georgie. "Your mom is so awesome. I wish my mom did stuff like that. I bet my mom hasn't even *heard* of the Cyber Queens. Can she get the rest of us tickets?"

"Don't think so," I replied. "I think she got the last ones."

"Take your digital camera," said Hannah. "Take lots of pictures to show us."

"Sure," I said.

I felt guilty when the bell rang for afternoon classes. Not only did I not have tickets for the Cyber Queens, but I don't have a digital camera either, even though I'd told everyone that my grandma had gotten me one as an early birthday present. I lied. I don't really like doing it, but sometimes it's necessary. I have to make things up so that they don't think that I'm a total loser. My friends have rich parents who buy them all the latest stuff: iPods, cell phones with cameras, computer games, designer clothes. They've all got their own TVs *and* their own computers in their bedrooms. I don't even have my own bedroom. Not even my own bed. Not really. I have to share a room and a bunk bed with my sister, Andrea. Sometimes I sleep on the downstairs sofa just to get a bit of space, although even then I have to share it—with our cats, Midnight and Meatloaf. (My brother Will named them. Midnight's black, and Meatloaf is a dark tabby.)

Anyway, my friends would surely dump me if they knew the truth about my situation and how poor we really are compared to them. When we first all started hanging out together as a group at the beginning of this year, to dissuade them from coming over, I told them that our house was being redecorated from top to bottom—kitchen, bathroom, the whole thing. I keep telling the girls that we're having "nightmares" with the workers, who keep letting us down. It's an expression that I've heard their parents use a million times.

So far, they haven't been over a lot, but when they have been, my excuses have worked, because the fact is, our house does look like it's in the middle of being redecorated. The walls are patchy with daubs of paint here and there where we decided to try out some paint samples but there wasn't enough cash to buy the paint. There are no carpets on the stairs. The carpets that are down on the floor are worn. There are floorboards up here and there. The whole place looks like it needs to be ripped out and redone from top to toe, so my story has never met with any questions.

Sometimes I think that Georgie may have caught on, but she's never come out and said anything, not yet anyway. It can be stressful on the rare occasions when the girls do come over since I'm afraid that Andrea, Will, or Dan might blow my cover. Instead, I try and make sure that we hang out at Megan, Hannah, or Georgie's houses. I tell them that the floor's up again or the water's off or something. They're so sympathetic that I feel rotten, especially since Georgie seems to like coming to our house, and she always brings something with her, like some fab muffins or expensive chocolate cookies or elderflower juice (my fave).

All my friends are kind. They invite me to sleep over at their houses when I lay on the construction nightmare scenario really thick—like last week I said that a plumber had caused a burst pipe and there was water everywhere. I like going to Georgie's place the best. It's awesome. They have five bedrooms at her house for just her and her mom. *Five.* And seeing as Georgie is an only child, that means that they have three spare. *Three*. I wish I could go and live with her sometimes, although I know deep down that I'd miss my family and especially the cats. Her house is like a palace compared to where I live; I feel like a princess when I'm there, and her mom never interferes with her life. Not like my house. No privacy there. Not even in the bathroom, as there is always someone knocking on the door telling whoever is in there to hurry up.

Some days, like today, being poor stinks. It is Friday. May 12th. The whole world would be out enjoying the early summer sun this evening. Certainly half of our school would be. Everyone down at the local theater to watch a movie and hang out. Some of the older girls from our school would also be there, showing off the fab new outfits they'd just got. There would probably even be some boys there from Marborough High down the road. And I'd have to miss out on the whole outing because I haven't got enough money to go.

As we got up to go back into school, there was a sudden blast of wind, blowing up dust and debris from the playground.

"Whoa," said Georgie as her skirt billowed up. "Where's that come from?"

"Dunno," said Meg, "but let's run."

In an instant, more papers and candy wrappers began to blow in a mini tornado around the playground as the kids headed back inside. A piece of paper flew toward me and stuck to my hand. I flicked it off, but it fluttered back again, and we all laughed, because after I brushed it off for the second time, it seemed to follow me as we headed back to the classroom. It was dancing along behind me, and just before I reached the door, it blew right up until it covered my face so that I couldn't see.

"Bleurgh," I blustered as I pulled it away from my eyes.

"Maybe it's meant for you," said Megan, taking the paper away from me. "Let's see what it is."

"Yeah, right," I said. "Maybe it's a message from a fairy." I was teasing her because last year she was into fairies and angels, and her bedroom was covered with posters of them.

"What does it say?" asked Hannah.

Megan scanned the paper. "Dear Tori, You are to go to the bluebell dell at midnight on Friday night . . ."

I punched her arm playfully. I knew she was making that up. "What does it really say?"

"It looks like some sort of promotion-type thing," she replied. "Um . . . advertising local businesses kind of thing. A beauty salon in Osbury. A café/deli. An astrology website. Stuff like that."

"I'll chuck it," I said and took it to put it in the garbage can in the corner of the playground. As I threw it away, there was a flash of lightning and then a rumble of thunder in the distance. I glanced up. The sky had darkened, threatening sudden rain, so I raced back to join the others at the door.

"The fairies are angry that you threw away their business promotion," joked Georgie.

"Yeah, right. Fairies and elves are alive and well and have taken over Osbury." I laughed back.

Seconds later, the sky opened, and rain pelted down, so we darted inside as quick as we could.

"Phew," I said as we raced along the corridors. "Just made it."

As we settled into class, our teacher, Miss Wilkins, was busy closing the windows that had been open earlier in the morning. The rain continued pouring down, and the wind was still whipping up debris outside. As she reached the last window at the back of the class near my desk, a piece of paper blew in. It sailed right across the classroom and landed *plonk* in front of me.

Meg, Hannah, and Georgie turned to look. I glanced down. It was the same piece of paper that had been following me in the playground! Beauty salon, deli, astrology website . . .

Maybe Megan was right and there were fairies and guardian angels out there. Maybe this was a message from one of them in code or something. *Yeah. And I'm the richest girl in the world*, I thought. However, the paper arriving in front of me did make me wonder. I didn't believe in fairyland like Meg did, but I *did* believe that some things are meant to be. Like fate. Or destiny. And *this* was a coincidence. I couldn't deny that. Maybe it *was* meant for me. I was about to put the paper in my backpack to look at it more carefully later when Miss Wilkins closed the last window and turned back to the class. As she did, she saw the paper that had landed on my desk.

"That garbage is blowing everywhere!" she said as she picked it up, ripped it into tiny pieces, and took it to the front of the room, where she threw it away. "Such a nuisance."

Oh, no, I thought as I watched her do it. *There goes the message about my destiny—straight into the trash!*

Chapter Two

Movie night

"I'm sitting there. I got the DVDs," said Will as he shoved Dan off the most comfortable chair in our living room. It's red and velvety, with thick, plush cushions. Okay, it's a little bit worn on the arms and some stuffing's coming out of it around the back, but you can sink right into it like it's made out of marshmallows. Will found it in a Dumpster last summer and dragged it back here with the help of a few of his friends.

"No. *I'm* sitting there," Dan insisted. "It's *my* turn. You sat there last night."

After a bit more pushing and shoving, they ended up wrestling on the floor and pulling each other's hair.

"Welcome to my world," I said to no one in particular. I stepped over them with the bowl of popcorn I'd just made and sat on the chair in question. "Movie time," I said as I turned on the TV.

They both sat up and stared at me in amazement when they saw that I was sitting in the prize chair. For a moment, we all looked at each other and then burst out laughing. We did look silly. I was dressed in black with a tall hat in a wicked witch outfit, and Dan and Will were dressed as devils, complete with horns and vampire teeth. Dressing up appropriately to watch a movie on Friday night has been a tradition in our house since we were little. Mom started it, and it makes it more fun. We have a huge trunk of assorted costumes that Mom has either made or that have been collected from various garage sales over the years. Witches, wizards, clowns, gorillas, giant vegetables—you name it, and it's probably in the trunk. Aunt Phoebe, Uncle Kev, Aunt Pat, and Uncle Ernie have all contributed to the trunk and bring stuff back from their vacations. They also like to get in costume if they come over to watch a DVD at our house.

Dan was about to make a dive at me, but I grinned at him and held up my magic wand. "Talk to the wand, because the face ain't listening."

"But it's *my* turn," he said again.

I almost gave in because he looked so put out. But I didn't.

"Life is tough, oh small and puny one," I said. (Dan hates being called that, as he is quite small for his age.) "I will tell Mom that you skipped soccer practice last Saturday if you don't let me sit here. Now sit on the sofa, shut up, and let's watch the DVD."

"You wouldn't."

"Try me."

"It's my chair. I brought it back here, so I should be the one to sit in it *all* the time," said Will, who looked as if he was about to wrestle me, too. I pulled out my blackmail card on him.

"Oh, really? Well, if you don't let me sit here, I will tell my friend Georgia that you like her." (What Will doesn't know is that I have a sneaking suspicion that Georgie likes him back. I will save that piece of information for another night when it might come in handy.) Will is a looker. Lots of girls at our school like him. He's got typical rock-star good looks. A handsome face with even features and a slim body. And no zits (big plus). Even though he's my brother, I can see that he's attractive. Dan's cute too, with a wide mouth and the green eyes that we have all inherited from our mom. Dan will be a babe magnet when he's older. At the moment, though, he's not remotely interested in girls. He thinks they're for pushing, teasing, or hair pulling, and he hates kissing scenes in movies. He says that watching people suck face makes him want to throw up.

Dan shrugged and then got up to slump on the sofa, and a moment later, Will joined him, along with Meatloaf and Midnight, who took their places on the boys' knees. The cats like a good movie too.

"Correct response," I said with a big smile. Will stuck out his tongue at me. I love my brothers, really, and their fighting is rarely serious. Just boys being stupid boys.

I used to wonder how Dad would have dealt with their endless fights and messing around, but I hardly think about him anymore. It's a waste of time. He clearly isn't coming back anytime soon. He left when I was ten. Went back to Australia, leaving Mom with the four of us. She sat us all down after he'd left and said that it had been on the cards for years (like we didn't already know). No one was to blame, and they should never have gotten married in the first place since they were such different types of people (ditto— we could hear their endless arguments through the ceiling; they could never agree about anything). I could accept that they were incompatible. I've watched the soaps on TV. I know what goes down, but personally I don't see why he had to go quite so far away, especially when he had the four of us. If he ever took an "Abandon Your Kids" test, he'd get an A-plus. Okay, so he didn't get along with Mom, but what about Andrea, Dan, Will, and me? We got along. Yeah, sometimes he was moody and unpredictable, and I didn't like that, and I *hated* it when he and Mom argued, but he was my dad, and you only get one of them. I missed him, and when he first left, it hit me hard. I felt like a major reject. Like if my own *dad* didn't want me, then no one else would.

I don't let myself think about stuff like that anymore now, though. It hurts too much. I put it in a box in my head and locked it. Mom has been great. She tries really hard, but for all of her positive attitude, she hasn't found it easy as a single mother. Not enough money. Her sisters, Phoebe and Pat, and their husbands have been fab and are in and out most days to lend a hand where they can. I love them a lot and know that they love me, too. They don't have kids of their own and have sort of adopted us. When they're around, I don't have that reject feeling. They make me feel like I matter. Dad sends some money every now and then, but not often, because, from his letters, it doesn't sound like he has a job yet. That was one of the major sources of the arguments. Mom worked day and night. Dad talked about it but always seemed to have an excuse as to why it wasn't happening.

"Pass me the DVD remote," I said as I spied it on the table.

"You get it," said Dan. "I'm not your slave."

"Yes, you are," I said.

"Oh, give me a break," said Will. He snatched up the remote and passed it to me. "I'll get it. Here.

Sometimes you're so lazy, Tori."

"So?" I said and kicked off my shoes. "Lazy is good. Now let the entertainment begin." With a flourish of the remote control, I turned on the DVD. We had popcorn and soda. Aunt Phoebe and Uncle Kev would come by later with pizza. It was going to be a fun evening, despite my earlier disappointment at not being able to go out with my friends.

On the way home from school, I had decided to make the most of the evening and not to sulk about not being able to go out. I'm not a miserable person usually. Just frustrated sometimes. But no point in dwelling on what can't be changed, I decided. Andrea was out at her *book* club sleepover—yes, book club sleepover. She is 17 years old. It is Friday night, and she would rather sit around discussing books at a sleepover than try out new makeup or gossip or talk about boys or watch a good movie. That is how sad my sister is. Sometimes I think she isn't actually a member of our family. She doesn't look like the rest of us. She has pale skin and blond, wispy hair and blue eyes. The rest of us are dark with green eyes. So, anyway, it was just me and the boys. And the cats (who are also dark with green eyes).

The DVDs that Will had borrowed were horror movies (hence our scary costumes), and as the evening went on, we had a good laugh seeing who got spooked the most. It was Dan, as usual. He's been such a sissy since some old guy at the local train station told him about ghosts who appear outside people's windows just before they die and wail, "The day is for the living, and the night is for the dead."

When he went in to make us some hot chocolate (he *is* our slave, as he is the youngest at 11), Will and I sneaked outside and began wailing outside the kitchen window. It was hysterical. Dan turned white and almost dropped the mug he had in his hand. Then Will blew it by laughing, and Dan looked out the window and saw us doing our cross-eyed zombie walk around the clothesline out there. He wasn't amused.

Personally, I don't think there's any such things as ghosts or zombies, but Dan does, and he was really mad at us. He doesn't mind dressing up as a vampire, but he doesn't like to think that there might be a real one behind the hedge in our backyard. He stormed upstairs and wouldn't come out of his room. We had to beg him in the end. We had to get down on our knees in the corridor outside the room that he shares with Will and plead. Dan can be so stubborn and moody sometimes. Especially if he thinks that people are making fun of him. Aunt Phoebe and Uncle Kev arrived with food supplies soon after, and that brought him down. He couldn't resist the allure of a double-cheese pizza. And he couldn't help but smile when he saw what idiots they looked like in their evil goblin masks.

Mom got home at 11:30, just after Aunt Phoebe and Uncle Kev had left.

"What are you still doing up?" she asked when she saw us all sitting around watching TV. "It's way past your bedtime."

"Oh, come on, Mom—it's Friday night. No school tomorrow," said Will.

"And I was waiting up for you," I said and got up from the sofa and gave her a hug. "Let me go and make you a grilled cheese and some hot chocolate."

"And one for me," said Dan.

"And me," called Will.

"Make your own," I called back as I went into the kitchen and got out mugs for all of us. "And, anyway, you've just stuffed your faces with pizza."

I like to make a fuss over Mom when she gets home. She works so hard, and she looked tired tonight. She often has lately, but, then, who wouldn't if they had to work three jobs? She has no time to take care of her appearance anymore, and she always just shoves her hair back in a headband and wears old T-shirts and sweatpants. I remember years ago when her hair looked stylish and glossy and her clothes were pretty and she wore some jewelry. That

25

was when she only had one job, and that was part-time at the library. Now all she does is work. During the daytime on Monday to Friday, she works as a receptionist at the local vet's. Most evenings, she does cleaning jobs for an agency that sends her to places like the stadium—which is where she's been tonight. If there's been a big game on, she doesn't get home until one. Tonight, though, it was the Cyber Queens concert, and she will have brought me back some tickets since she knows that I like to collect concert tickets in my scrapbook with the green-and-gold Chinese cover. It wasn't totally a lie that I told Georgie about having tickets. Just that I didn't get them until the show was *over*.

Mom's third job is baking cakes for special occasions. She's totally amazing at it. She can make whatever anyone wants—like if someone works with computers, say, she can make their cake look like a PC. Or if someone is a photographer, she can make the cake look like a camera. She's done Superman cakes for little boys, pink heart cakes for Valentine's Day, cakes shaped like tennis rackets for tennis fans—whatever anyone wants. Sadly, she doesn't have much time for this job since the cleaning agency keeps calling.

"So how's your day been?" asked Mom as she picked up the mail from the hall table and followed me into the kitchen.

"Okay," I said. I didn't tell her about having to miss out on the Crazy Maisies' movie outing. I didn't want her feeling bad about stuff like that on top of everything else. For a few moments while I made her sandwich, I thought about asking if there was the slightest chance that I might be able to go on the school trip if I didn't have any allowance money for the next 15 years. The look on her face as she opened one of the letters stopped me.

"What is it?" I asked.

She took a deep breath. "Oh, nothing interesting. Another bill."

"Can you pay it?"

She nodded. "Just about. Don't you worry, Tori. We'll get by. We'll survive. We always do."

I couldn't help but sigh as I continued making her dinner. *Get by.* I wished we didn't just have to get by. I wished we didn't just have enough to survive. I wished our family could thrive. I wished Mom could have nice clothes again and not have to work so hard. And music-crazy Will could get an iPod and, for Dan, the bike he's wanted for ages. And I wished I could have things like Megan and Georgie and Hannah. I wanted to go out with them like normal girls my age. *Actually, no*, I suddenly thought. *I don't want to be normal. I want to be super filthy stupidly rich. I'd even buy Meatloaf and Midnight new collars. With diamonds on them!*

"What's the big sigh all about?" asked Mom, who, as usual, didn't miss a thing. "Everything okay with the Crazy Maisies?"

"Yeah. Fine," I said as I busied myself getting out a tray. I put all thoughts about Italy out of my mind and arranged the things on the tray so that they looked nice. I've learned to do this from Mom. She does her best to make the most ordinary things special, even if it's only by putting nice napkins or fresh flowers on the dining room table.

"By the way," she said with a grin as I put the tray with its folded Christmas napkin (it was all I could find) in front of her, "I have something you might be interested in."

She rummaged around in her bag and produced an envelope and held it out to me. "Here. Tomorrow night at the Bridgewater Hotel out near Osbury, they're hosting a charity event. I have some tickets if you want to go."

I tried to look enthusiastic, but a charity event? Big deal. Not.

Mom laughed when she saw my face. "Not just any charity event," she said. "It's a charity ball. Chance to glam up, and I know how much you like to do that. All the stars are going to be there. Take a look at the guest list."

I took the piece of paper from her and glanced down. Omigod! Topping the bill were the Dust Babies. Only my favorite band in the universe. And omigod, omi*god*, Alicia Bartley from my favorite soap. And . . . it can't be . . . Ewan Gregory from T4. He's sooooo gorgeous. My fantasy boy.

The list went on.

"This is like . . . *mega*," I finally managed to stutter. "And you're saying that I can go?"

Mom grinned and nodded. "Mrs. Jackson, the lady who's organizing it, she's really nice—remember her? I made her a swimming pool cake last year for her birthday. She asked me to make some of my special cakes for part of the auction and help her out a little. She asked if I'd like a couple of free tickets for anyone."

"But, Mom, this is awesome . . ." I said as I took in the rest of the names on the A-star list.

"I know, sweetie," she said. "Charity is big business these days. They all try to attract the big names. And it looks like it will be fun."

"I'll say."

"So you want to go?"

"Um . . . obviously."

Mom smiled. "Good. It's about time you had something special to look forward to, Tori."

This is so cool, I thought. *Okay, so Cinderella doesn't get to go to Italy. Or to the movies. But she gets to go to the ball. The hottest charity ball in history.* I couldn't wait to tell Hannah, Meg, and Georgie.

Chapter Three

Osbury

"Mom will be mad at you if she knows that you've been snooping in there," said Will, appearing behind me as I was going through Mom's closet on Saturday morning when I thought everyone was out.

I'd had every stitch of clothing that I owned out on the floor in my and Andrea's bedroom. And every stitch that Andrea owned too, as she was out at her chess club meeting. (She really is the queen of Dorksville. Interests: chess, books, science, and history. Bleurgh.) After I had exhausted our stuff, I went to look at Mom's.

"But she isn't going to find out, is she?" I said and attempted to grab Will's wrist and give him a Chinese burn. He was too quick for me and jabbed me in the stomach, causing me to curl over in pain. Oh, the joy of having brothers. I had hoped that he might have grown out of the wanting-to-torture-his-little-sister phase now that he'd turned 15, but apparently not.

"What will you give me not to tell her?" asked Will.

"A black eye," I said. "Now go away and leave me

alone. I have important business to conduct."

"Like what?"

"Like finding what I am going to wear for this big party tonight. It's hopeless, Will. I may even have to give the ticket to someone else."

"Why? I thought you were on cloud nine about going—chance to show off and stuff."

"I was, but, oh . . . you won't understand. You're a boy."

Will surveyed the pile of clothes that I'd put on the bed. "I do understand, actually. I'm not as stupid as you think. You don't know what to wear, and you want to look cool."

Hmm. Maybe he *wasn't* as stupid as I thought.

"Yeah . . . well . . . exactly. It's, like, really important. There will be some awesome people there, and you can bet anything that they'll be wearing all the latest designer stuff, not hand-me-downs that don't fit right. I've got nothing. I'm such a Discount Diva."

"Discount Diva?" asked Will.

"Someone who only has uncool clothes, you know, clothes that don't have brand names, designer stuff."

"Oh, that. So what? Don't you think it's whether something looks good or not that counts, not if it's got some expensive name on it? You must have something."

"Nothing that's nice enough. Only that silver top

that Mom got me last year from the Salvation Army, but it got all shiny and stretchy in the wash. Oh, why can't I have a sister who has style? A sister who has a closet full of cool clothes that I can borrow? She has as much dress sense as a dead dog. I, on the other hand, have fabulous taste."

"Fabulous doesn't always mean expensive," said Will.

"What do you know?"

"I've got eyes, don't I?" said Will as he made himself comfortable on Mom's bed. "And I've seen some girls look hot because of the way they wear what they've got on. Not because it cost a fortune. Anyway, why can't you borrow something from one of your rich friends? Georgie looks loaded. I bet she's got lots of stuff. Ask her."

"Once again, you poor, challenged-in-the-brain-department person, you don't understand."

"Yes, I do. You don't want her to know that we're poor. Don't think I don't know that you're ashamed of who we are and where we live and . . ."

I felt shocked that he'd think that, because not in a million, billion years would I be ashamed of him. "I am not! Shows what you know. Anyway, Mom had two tickets, and Andrea wasn't interested in going, so she said that I could ask a friend. So I asked Georgie. So there. That's why I don't want to borrow anything from her, because she will be wearing her nicest outfit herself."

"Bet she's got lots of other things. And you *are* ashamed of us. I've seen you when you're here with your friends. You can't get them out of the house fast enough."

"I'm *not* ashamed of us, Will. Honest. Not of who we are, just of where we live. I mean, look at it . . ." I said as I indicated the old-fashioned beige wallpaper. "I mean, if you saw Georgie's house, you'd understand."

Will shrugged. "I have friends who live in nice houses. So what? That's not why I hang out with them. Or them with me."

"Yeah, but you're a boy. What do boys care about nice things? All you care about are sports and computer games. For me, how things look matters."

Will looked at me sulkily. "I don't think you should care about stuff like that. What does it matter?"

"It matters a lot, *il stupido*—now get out and leave me alone."

"Hey," said Will as he got off Mom's bed. "If it's a charity ball, why don't you go to a thrift store? You might find something. You never know."

With that, he trudged off to his room, and after I'd exhausted Mom's closet, I began to think that his idea wasn't half bad. Sometimes people give away really nice stuff to thrift stores. I wouldn't go to our local store, though. They wouldn't have anything decent. I knew what was in there, as all our family are regulars. Mom gets most of our clothes in there. Andrea gets books, Will gets DVDs, Dan gets great computer games, and I get some good CDs. But clothes fit for a ball? No chance. The stuff in our local store was the sort of thing that even the flea markets didn't want. But there were other thrift stores in other areas. Areas where rich people lived. Suddenly I remembered the leaflet that had blown toward me on Friday. For stores in Osbury. It was the town closest to our school. A few new stores had opened there recently, and I was sure that one of them was a thrift store.

After leaving a note for Mom, I ran as fast as I could to the bus stop and took the bus to Osbury. It was the most upmarket town in our area. If there were going to be designer giveaways anywhere, then that would be the place.

Half an hour later, I got off the bus and scanned the row of stores across from the bus stop. *Result!* I thought. *There's the thrift store.*

I was about to make my way across the street when someone tapped me on the shoulder. I turned to find the most stunning-looking woman I had ever seen. She didn't look like a local; in fact, she looked like a celebrity and in her early 20s, although I was never very good at judging people's ages. I couldn't help but stare at her—she looked like she'd just stepped out of the pages of *Vogue* magazine. She had blue eyes, like the sky on the clearest day in the summer, a perfect heart-shaped face, long, blond hair, whiter-than-white teeth, and she was wearing the most fabulicious white T-shirt and jeans with studs down the sides. I could tell that they cost megabucks. *And she smells amazing*, I thought as her perfume wafted toward me on the breeze. It was sweet but delicate, like the scent of white roses after it rained.

She handed me a piece of paper and said in a Southern accent, "I think this is yours, darlin'."

I glanced down at it. Omigod! It was the same as the paper that had blown my way at school yesterday.

"Oh! But . . . this . . . I . . . um . . ." I began.

But the lady had already turned and was heading in the opposite direction. "Don't lose it this time," she called over her shoulder and then gave me a wave as she walked away.

I looked at the paper again. *Weird*, I thought. *Why did she give it to me? Did she think I had dropped it?* Whatever the reason, it seemed like I really was supposed to have it. This was the third time it had come to me. I decided to take a closer look later, so I stuffed it inside my pocket and crossed the street to the store.

As soon as I got inside, I started rummaging through the racks. There were a few things that looked promising, and after 15 minutes I had a bunch of outfits to try on. Even if they didn't fit perfectly, I could probably alter them since I'm good at adapting clothes. Art is one of my best subjects at school, and being creative seems to come easy. Feeling more positive than I had all day, I went into the changing room.

The first outfit was a midlength black dress in a floaty voile-type material. I slipped it over my head and looked in the mirror.

Waaaay too big. And the color drained me. Even if I raced home and altered it on Mom's sewing machine, it wasn't going to work.

The second was a pink satin dress.

Yuck. I looked like a bridesmaid, and the material was way too shiny. Not flattering at all.

The third one was a pale mushroom color but looked sophisticated.

Until I got it on, that is. It was *waaaay* too long. I looked like a kid in her mom's dress. And once again, the color made me look washed out.

The fourth looked like it might be perfect. Short with a halter neckline. Peacock blue. I read somewhere that it's a good color for people with green eyes like me.

I held my breath and squeezed into it. Way too tight. Only a nine year old would fit into it.

Ah, well, I thought as I reached for the fifth one, a short white Lycra dress, *this looks like it might fit.*

It did. It was perfect. I did a twirl. And then I saw the back. It had a huge nasty stain, like someone had spilled red wine down the back. No wonder its previous owner had given it away.

I felt so disappointed as I got dressed. Will's great idea wasn't going to work. I put the clothes back on the rack and then had another rummage through, but found nothing, only way old-fashioned stuff that I wouldn't be seen dead in. I had picked out all of the best pieces already.

I checked my watch. Two o'clock. The party started at 6:30, and I still had nothing to wear, but no way could I go in my ratty old clothes from last year. I'd have to think up some excuse to tell Georgie why I couldn't go.

I left the store and crossed the street to the bus stop, where I got out the leaflet that I'd been given earlier. I took a closer look to try and figure out why it had come to me. I scanned both sides. It advertised a deli. Yes, I could see that across the street. A beauty salon, Pentangle. Yes, I could see that, too. An Internet café. Hmm. Hadn't noticed that before.

It also gave an address for a website about astrology. I liked reading about stuff like that. All of us Crazy Maisies did. We regularly read our horoscope in our magazines. Maybe my horoscope this month had something special to tell me. Maybe something about my predicament—a dance to go to but nothing to wear.

I decided that I'd take a look at the site when I got home if Dan and Will weren't hogging the computer, that is, if it was even working (it was an old one that Uncle Ernie had given us when he bought a new model for his own use. If it wasn't for him, we'd be totally in the last century, because as well as donating the PC to us as a special Christmas present for the whole family, he said he'd pay for our Internet connection.).

Then I had a flash of inspiration. An Internet café was right across from me. That meant computers. A computer that I could actually use without having to wait until the Brothers Grimm, Dan and Will, got off it. Bliss. And I could look up the astrology website right now and find out what my destiny for the month was.

I looked again at the Internet café. It was up at the end of the row, and it looked like it was open, as I could see people moving around inside. The storefront was painted in bright blue, silver, and turquoise. I crossed the street and peered in the window. *Whoa. Space-age city*, I thought as I took in the futuristic décor inside. The front half seemed to be a store selling party stuff and novelty items, but at the back, I could see several geek-type people sitting at computers, and at the very back was a counter selling drinks in bright fluorescent glasses. It looked like a cool place, so I opened the door and ventured inside.

Gentle music floated out through loudspeakers in the corners. Choirs of angels singing. Looking around, I felt like I'd entered some kind of spaceship. *Jeez*, I thought, *I've walked onto the set of a freaking* Star Trek *movie*. To the left of the door was a chrome counter, behind which was the most extraordinary-looking person. He had silver spiked-up hair and was dressed in an electric blue Lycra jumpsuit and high silver platform boots. Very space age meets punk.

"Hey," he said as soon as he saw me. "Computers are in the back. Use the one on the right."

"But . . ." I was about to ask how he knew that I wanted to use one of the computers but then rationalized that probably most people who went in there did so, because, like me, they didn't have access to one at home.

"Thanks," I said and made my way to the back of the store.

I sat down in front of the screen, and the space

40

punk man came over and stood behind me. "Know how to use it?"

I glanced at the screen. "Think so."

"Internet you want, right?"

I nodded. "How much?"

"Free for you."

"Free?"

"Special promotion," he said as he leaned over and moved the mouse so that the Internet opened up. "Just type in the site you want."

"Thanks," I said.

"I'm Uri," he said. "Just let me know if you need anything." Then he winked and drifted off to help a new customer, a lady in her 20s, who had sat down a few feet away. I couldn't help but notice that when she asked how much it was to use the Internet, Uri said, "One dollar an hour," and took her money! *Strange*, I thought and then decided that maybe it was a promotion for teenagers or something.

I got out the leaflet, typed in the website address, and waited for it to load. After a few moments, the screen appeared like a dark night sky. *Fitting for an astrology site*, I thought as soft, tinkling music accompanied the unfolding picture.

A scroll floated down from the right-hand corner of the screen and uncurled itself to reveal a form asking for my name and date, time, and place of birth. *Freaking fairy farts*, I thought. *I don't know the time I was born.* I got out my phone and called Mom. Luckily, she picked up.

"Hey, what time was I born, Mom?"

"Two-fifteen in the morning," she said. "Why?"

"Tell you later," I said and hung up.

I typed in the time and sat back to wait for it to give me my horoscope. I liked being in the café. It had a tranquil atmosphere, like it was a space station hovering just outside Earth. Everyone working away quietly. The angelic music playing from the loudspeakers. Very peaceful . . .

Suddenly a trumpet fanfare BLASTED out of the computer. Really LOUD. I almost jumped out of my seat and so did a number of the computer geeks sitting nearby.

"Shhh," shushed one of them and gave me a dirty look.

"Not my fault," I whispered back. "*I* didn't know that it was going to do that!"

But the noise was getting louder and louder.

"Congratulations," said a neon message flashing on the screen. "You are this month's Zodiac Girl."

And the trumpet got even louder, like the person playing it was bursting their cheeks, lungs, liver, and kidneys to hit the highest note.

I glanced around. Everyone in the café was staring

at me.

"Quiet," shushed another geek.

"Sorry," I called back to him. "It's one of those pop-up things. I'll get rid of it."

Desperately, I scanned the keyboard for some kind of volume control. There it was up at the top. I pressed it as fast as I could, but the music continued to get even louder. Everyone was still staring at me, including Uri, who was grinning his head off.

"Help," I mouthed to him.

He gave me the thumbs-up and clapped his hands for attention. "Quiet, everyone, and let's hear it for this month's Zodiac Girl. Hip, hip, hooray."

As he led the cheers, a few of the geeks looked at him as if he was crazy.

"What are you doing?" I asked when he came over. "I don't want to disturb anyone any more than I already have. Please turn the sound off and get rid of that pop-up thingy that's flashing. I can't stop it."

"But you're this month's Zodiac Girl," said Uri. "Why would you want to get rid of it? It's fantastic. Don't you realize what it means?"

"No, I don't," I whispered. "Please, please turn the noise off. Everyone's staring."

Uri typed in something, and the sound went off. "There you are. So. How do you feel?"

"About what?"

"Being a Zodiac Girl this month."

"Feel? Zodiac Girl? Nothing. I don't know what it means, and anyway, isn't everyone who goes to this site a Zodiac Girl? It's some kind of promotion thing, isn't it?"

"Heavens, no. There's only one Zodiac Girl a month. Just you. And it means, my dear," he said as he read the screen and saw my name, "that you, Tori, have a *great* month ahead of you. Well, hopefully great. It can go either way, depending on what you make of it. But all sorts of surprises are in store. Hmm. Let me see. So your sun is in Taurus? Tauruses are ruled by Venus, so that means you get Nessa as your guardian. Lucky you. She's faaaabulous. A goddess. You'll love her."

"Guardian? But . . . I don't want a guardian. I have a mom and a dad, too, although he doesn't live with us . . . what I'm trying to say is that I don't need anyone to take care of me, so you can tell this Nessa that she won't be needed."

Uri laughed. "Tell her yourself. She'll be in touch—you can count on that."

I was starting to feel spooked. Like someone was following me. First the paper blowing at me in the school playground. Then the beautiful lady handing the *same* paper to me, and now this. Fairies, angels, or not, Megan could keep them. I got up to go. "Right.

Okay. Thanks. Got to go now."

Uri leaned over to look at the screen. "You can ignore it if you want. Some do. Some people are afraid of the unknown and what they don't understand, but . . ." he seemed to be scanning my birth chart. "No. Yours is not the chart of a coward."

Well, I'm feeling decidedly cowardly now, I thought as I made my way to the door. As I opened it to leave, Uri called out, "There's a message on here for you, Zodiac Girl. Go back to where you have been, and you will find what you seek."

"Okay. Yes. Thank you. Bye," I stuttered as I shut the door behind me. Like, what in the world was that supposed to mean? Sometimes computer people can be way weird, and this one took the cake. *I want to go home*, I thought. *Safe. Planet Earth. Sofa. TV. Normal.*

On the way back to the bus stop, I passed the thrift store again. As I glanced in the window, I noticed that the old lady in there was getting some things out of a garbage bag and hanging them on the rack behind the counter. One of the items caught my eye.

Short. Floaty voile material. Halter neck. With teeny-weeny coral, primrose, and black flowers. Really pretty.

I had to go back in.

"Excuse me," I said as I approached the lady behind the counter and pointed at the dress. "Um

45

. . . is that for sale?"

She nodded and smiled. "It is. Looks like it's never been worn, and it's just about your size too. It's just come in. Want to try it on?"

She handed me the dress, and I took a quick glance at the label. Suzie Tsang. Omigod! I had read about her in one of my magazines last week. (Dan gets them for me. He does a paper route in a wealthy area, and on recycling day, he brings me back all the copies of *Vogue* and *Cosmo*.) So I knew Suzie Tsang was only the hottest new designer in the country.

"Um . . . how much is it?" I asked the lady.

"How much for this, Dora?" the lady called to someone in a back room. She held up the dress.

"Not much fabric, is there?" said a second white-haired lady appearing at the door. "Oh, give us a dollar for it if it fits you."

One dollar for a Suzie Tsang dress! If only they knew. These dresses went for four or five hundred dollars in the stores in New York City. I couldn't believe my luck. A dress like that, and I'd have change left over from the $4.50 I had in my wallet!

Please, please, please let it fit, I begged the patron saint of thrift stores as I went back into the changing room.

The angels, fairies, saints, and leprechauns were smiling on me. The dress fit like it had been specially made for me. It couldn't have looked more perfect. I could go to the ball, and I didn't have to be a Discount Diva after all.

I got dressed, made my purchase, and almost danced back to the bus stop. The sun was shining, and I felt fantastic.

Only on the way back did I remember the message for me that Uri had read from the astrology site. "Go back to where you have been, and you will find what you seek."

Could it have meant go back to the store? Go and buy the dress? Whatever. Yahoo! Something was going my way. I had a great new dress. Maybe it was in the stars that things were looking up after all.

Chapter Four

Party time!

Back at home, I went into a frenzy of getting ready for the charity ball. I had a "steps to beauty" list that I'd cut out of my *Star Girl* magazine last year in case I ever got invited to an event like this, but I never dreamed that it would happen so soon.

My list went:

Bathe: in my strawberry bubble bath that Mom got me for Christmas.

Exfoliate: with my mango scrub (present from Aunt Phoebe).

Moisturize: with apple body lotion.

Wash and condition my hair: with my blueberry shampoo and conditioner.

"Poo," said Dan when I came out of the bathroom. "You smell like a fruit salad."

I didn't react. I was having fun, and neither the fact that the boys had left water in the soap dish so that it was slimy, nor the fact that they'd left wet towels on the bathroom floor after their soccer practice, could ruin my mood. My world was good.

our ride, and even though I was, I wouldn't have wanted to offend them.

"You go on in, sweetie," said Mom when we stopped outside the kitchens at the back. "Go and find Georgie, and I'll see you later."

I hopped out as quick as I could and raced around to the front. It was a media frenzy as limos drove up, celebrities got out, and flashbulbs went off as the paparazzi called at them to look their way while they took photos. *Lucky that it's a warm evening*, I thought, *so everyone can really show off their fab outfits and not have to hide them underneath their coats.*

"Hey, Tori," I heard a familiar voice call.

It was Georgie to my right. She looked great in a soft blue mini dress and her hair up with little silver sparkles in it.

We did a quick *muwah, muwah* air kiss to the left, air kiss to the right (the way rich ladies do when they meet up in town).

"You look amazing," I said as I stepped back.

"Thanks. You do too, and wow, I so love your dress. Is it new?"

I nodded. "Yeah. Thanks. It's a Suzie Tsang. Mom got it for me on her last trip to New York."

"Suzie Tsang? Omigod. I love her stuff. It must have cost a fortune."

"You'd be shocked if you knew," I said and gave

her my best modest look.

All further talk about our outfits was cut short as another limo pulled up, and the photographers went crazy.

"Oh, wow!" said Georgie. "Look. It's Marsha Johnson from TV!"

Whoever said that money can't buy happiness? They had clearly never been to an event like this, I thought as we stood and watched as famous guest after famous guest arrived, smiled for the cameras, and then went inside. I couldn't believe that I was really going to be in there with them, but yes, we showed our tickets to the security man on the steps, and he waved us through with the rest of them.

Freaking awesome, I thought as we stepped inside the vast reception hall. There was so much to look at and take in. Flower arrangements as big as a bus. Marble pillars that looked like the real thing, not that fake plastic kind you can buy at Home Depot. Glittering chandeliers with a million candle bulbs shimmering light. So many people all dressed in their best outfits, the sound of chattering, laughing, champagne corks popping, glasses clinking. Georgie and I had a great time watching and gossiping about the ones who had no dress sense and drooling over those who'd gotten it right. In the main ballroom, disco music was playing and strobe lights flashing, and already a few people were up dancing. In another small hall, we could see that there were tables groaning with food, and at the back was a small stage where I spotted Mom laying out her cakes.

"Should we go and get something?" asked Georgie as she peeked in. "I'm starving."

I quickly steered her away. I didn't want her to know that Mom was working in there and was not a guest.

"I'll go and get us a drink and something to nibble on," I said. "I'll bring it to you in the dance room. You go and check out if there are any cute boys in there."

"Good plan," said Georgie, and she disappeared off into the disco.

As I went in to get the drinks, Mom spotted me, and I gave her a wave but didn't go over—she looked busy anyhow. As I got the drinks, I noticed Sonia Marks and Chloe Philips from ninth grade at the other end of the table. Sonia pointed at me and then put her hand to her friend's ear and whispered something. Chloe whipped around and stared at me, and then they both started laughing. Whatever they'd said wasn't nice. I could tell. *Maybe they know that my mom is part of the staff and I don't really belong here*, I thought and turned my back on them quickly.

On the way back through to the disco, I noticed everyone turn to look at someone who had just arrived. Thinking that it must be another celebrity, I turned to look as well. For a moment, I was blinded as flashbulb after flashbulb blasted off. When my eyes adjusted, I saw that it was a couple who had arrived. *Freaking incredible, do they look the business*, I thought as I stared along with the others gaping at them. *Pure gossip-magazine material.* The lady looked familiar. As my eyes focused properly, I realized that it was the beautiful woman who had given me the leaflet this morning in Osbury! She was on the arm of a man who seemed like he'd just walked off a movie set in Hollywood. She looked like a goddess dressed in an off-the-shoulder, long, Grecian-style ivory dress; her hair was up, and she was wearing silver star earrings. And he looked like a god. Tall, handsome, suntanned, with a mane of shoulder-length, black, wavy hair and with the same whiter-than-white teeth that the lady had. They radiated the cool factor like they ate charisma flakes for breakfast. Everyone was staring at them, both men and women alike. The lady looked around the room and waved at someone in my direction.

I turned to see who, but there was no one behind me. She waved again. Omigod. Was she waving at *me*? She couldn't be. But she was. She was even coming over!

She stopped in front of me and smiled. "Hey, Tori,"

she said. "It is Tori, isn't it? I thought I might see you here. I'm Nessa."

I was so shocked that I stood there doing my best goldfish impression. Why was she talking to me? Everyone was watching. But Nessa, *Nessa*? I had heard that name somewhere, and I recognized the scent—white roses and rain. Where? *Where*? I urged my brain to get into gear. Oh, yes. Nessa. It was the name of the person that the captain of the space-age lunatics' shop, Uri, had said was my guardian. He *couldn't* have meant this lady, could he? No way. She looked like a famous person. *People* magazine famous. And not crazy the way Uri looked. And *certainly* not some sad teenager's guardian.

When I finally got my bottom lip up off the floor and got my mouth to work, I said, "Hi. Um. Yes. I'm Tori."

"My Zodiac Girl," she said with a smile. "Tori Taylor. Taurus. I saw your chart."

With the excitement of coming to the dance, until now I'd forgotten about the strange announcement from the computer this afternoon. I certainly didn't think I'd hear any more about it, as I thought it was some computer pop-up thing that appeared whenever anybody went to the astrology site that I'd typed in. No big deal. But, hey, if it meant that this amazing woman was going to talk to me, I didn't mind. People were still watching us. *Famous by association. I can do that*, I thought as I shifted around on my feet and tried to look cool. People were actually looking at me as if I might be somebody.

"Yes, um, that's me, Zodiac Girl," I said and gave her a smile. "Tori is short for Victoria. All my friends call me that. Tori, that is, not Victoria."

"Then I will too," said Nessa, "because I hope that we will be friends."

Friends with someone like her! That would be awesome, I thought, so I gave her what I hoped was my most winning smile.

Before we could talk any more, an old man with a white beard appeared, gave me what I can only describe as a "what kind of hole did you crawl out of?" look, and pulled her away so that I didn't have a chance to ask her anything more about Zodiac Girls or guardians.

The rest of the evening went by in a blur. Cute waiters brought around trays of canapés and drinks, and Georgie and I stuffed our faces on the sweet ones. They were way tasty: mini chocolate cakes with raspberry sauce, teeny-weeny lime cheesecakes, and itty-bitty pancakes with maple syrup. Yumbolicious. After the nibbles, we had such a laugh in the disco. We went through the repertoire of dances that we had practiced on various sleepovers with Meg and Hannah. Our range went from Russian Cossack dancing (which I was awful at because I kept falling over when we had to do the "balance on one leg while kicking out with the other" part) to tango to belly dancing to line dancing to ballet to hula. I think some people thought that we were totally crazy, but we didn't care. We were having such a good time, and a cute-looking boy with dark, floppy hair even asked me to dance with him and joined in with gusto as we did our "dances from around the globe." *This is the life for me*, I thought as we square-danced around the dance floor. *I was born for the high life.*

Toward the end of the evening, we drifted out into an adjacent hall where the handsome man who had arrived with Nessa was introduced as Mr. Sonny Olympus, otherwise known as Mr. O. He got up to start an auction, and I could see people nudging each other and whispering as the bidding got under way. I could tell immediately that it wasn't in a nasty way like Chloe and Sonia from our school had been talking about me. I could see that it was in admiration.

Mr. O. was amazing and whipped up people's enthusiasm so that they were really going for it in attempts to outbid each other.

"And what am I bid for this fabulous gift basket from Brecknams and Stasons?" he asked in the kind of voice that sounded like one of those men who do the chocolate commercials on TV. Deep and velvety. "Let's start the bidding at one hundred dollars."

"Five million squillion," I said and pretended to put up my hand, but Georgie laughed and pushed it down.

"Two hundred," called a voice from the back.

And up and up it went until it reached 2,000! I did a quick calculation in my head. *That much money would feed our whole family for a year, I bet. There must be some filthy rich people here*, I thought, although looking around, I guessed that most of them just wanted to impress Mr. O. and get his attention, especially the women.

The auction continued, with people outbidding each other for all sorts of garbage. A bottle of old wine went for $250. *Crazy*, I thought, *especially when you can buy a brand-new one for around six dollars.*

"Just who is Mr. O.?" asked Georgie.

"He's an actor," I said in a deep actorlike voice. "I overheard someone saying that anyway."

"Thought so," she replied.

Next up were Mom's cakes, and when she took them up on the stage, I noticed that Mr. Olympus made a big fuss over her. She even blushed. I could see her cheeks flush from halfway down the hall. I felt pleased to see her looking like she was enjoying herself, and she looked pretty tonight in a red dress that Aunt Pat had lent her.

With Mr. O.'s help, the cakes were a huge hit and raised more than $100 each. I felt so proud of her and nudged Georgie.

"My mom made those," I said.

"Yeah, my mom does a lot of work for charities too," she replied.

I didn't tell her that Mom had been paid to make the cakes. It was Mrs. Jackson who actually donated them. Donating to charities was a luxury that our family couldn't afford at the moment.

"And now for the raffle," Mr. O. announced when the last item for auction was sold.

A fat bald man got up to join him onstage and held out a sack.

Mr. Olympus put his hand inside and pulled out a ticket. "And the winner of the picnic basket is number one hundred forty-four."

"That's me!" cried a lady with frizzy red hair at the front who made her way to the stage, where she was presented with her prize.

A few other people had their ticket numbers called, and they, too, went to collect their prizes.

"Let's go and get a drink," I said to Georgie, and we turned to go out of the auction room.

"And finally," said Mr. Olympus as he put his hand

inside the sack and pulled out a ticket, "the last prize. And the winner is . . . number twelve . . . and the ticket belongs to . . . Tori Taylor."

"Omigod," said Georgie, pulling me back. "That's you! I never saw you buy a ticket."

"I . . . I didn't," I said as she shoved me forward. *I haven't got one. Maybe Mom bought one for me*, I thought as I made my way to the stage.

Up on the stage, Mr. O. gave me a package. As I took it, he winked at me.

"But I don't have the ticket," I said.

"No matter," he said. "The package has your name on it. Tori Taylor."

I wasn't going to argue. "Okay. Wow, thanks," I said and raced back to join Georgie and unwrap it.

We ripped off the paper, and inside was the coolest cell phone that I had ever seen. It was so pretty, tiny, in a pale pearly green with a glittering jewel the color of an emerald set in it. I immediately put it up to my ear and did the Crazy Maisie catwalk strut out into the corridor and back.

"Wow," said Georgie. "That is the cutest phone I have ever seen. It's like it was made for a fairy princess or something. I wonder where it came from. I've definitely never seen one like it before. Oh, and look, there's something else."

At the bottom of the package was a small box. I

opened it to find a silver chain with a charm of some sort on it. When I looked closer, I saw that it was the zodiac sign for Taurus. *This night is just getting better and better*, I thought as I fastened the chain around my neck.

Just at that moment, Sonia and Chloe passed by, and Sonia bumped into me.

"Sorr*eeee*," she said in a fake way. "Wasn't looking where I was going."

I was sure that she'd done it on purpose.

Chloe looked me up and down. "Hi, Diva," she said and then snickered.

I felt a rush of panic. "I . . . My name is Tori, actually," I said.

"Yeah, right," said Sonia, and then she leaned forward and whispered in my ear. "But you're still a Discount Diva . . ."

I felt my stomach tighten and my face flush red. *Oh, God, no*, I thought. *Could she possibly know that I'd gotten my dress from the secondhand store?*

"What's your problem?" said Georgie, coming to my defense.

"Just ignore them," I said and began to pull her away. "It's nothing."

"Didn't you tell your friend?" said Sonia.

"Tell me what?" asked Georgie, squaring up to her.

"That your friend here is a Discount Diva," said Chloe.

"Don't you call her that," said Georgie.

"Why not? She is one. Your friend here can't afford to buy designer clothes unless she buys them in thrift stores."

"Um, excuse me. She's only wearing a Suzie Tsang," said Georgie. "You don't see too many of *those* in thrift stores, now, do you?"

Inwardly, I felt as if I was dying. This *couldn't* be happening.

Chloe burst out laughing. "No. You don't unless you go to Osbury. See, that dress used to belong to Sonia. She gave it to a thrift store earlier today, didn't you, Sonia?"

Sonia nodded.

"There are more places than thrift stores to buy dresses, you know," said Georgie. "Tell her, Tori. Tell her that your mom got it for you in New York."

"I . . . I . . ." I had no excuse and felt exposed and close to tears. "I . . ."

"You said it's a Suzie Tsang dress, right?" said Sonia.

I didn't say anything.

"Yeah," said Georgie. "So, what are you trying to say, Sonia?"

"So, Suzie Tsang is my aunt, and she made it for me specially for my fifteenth birthday, and your friend couldn't have bought it in New York, because she only made one, and that was for me. So there."

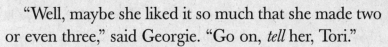

"Well, maybe she liked it so much that she made two or even three," said Georgie. "Go on, *tell* her, Tori."

But I still couldn't speak. I felt frozen from my toes to my tongue. Like someone had sprayed me with instant ice.

Sonia leaned over and pulled the back of the neck of my dress up. "Here," she said. "Look at the label. The hand-stitched label. It says, 'For Sonia.'"

"So why did you give it away?" asked Georgie, who looked like she'd like to hit Sonia.

Sonia feigned a yawn. "Oh, you know. I've worn it a few times now, so I'm bored with it. I don't really like wearing things that people have seen me in before. So passé, don't you think, to wear the same things over and over again? And Aunt Suzie's made me so many things over the years. I gave it to my mom to give away."

"So that some *poor* unfortunate soul could wear it, but I bet you never expected to see it turn up here, hey, Sonia?" added Chloe.

By now I felt my face was crimson. I felt that everyone in close proximity had heard what the girls were saying and was staring at me. I wanted the ground to open up and swallow me.

Sonia started singing in a slow, mocking voice, "Discount Divaaaa, Discount Divaaaa, Discount Divaaaa . . ."

Chloe joined in with her. "Discount Divaaaa, Discount Divaaaa, Discount Divaaaa . . ."

I felt so ashamed. Everyone *was* looking. Suddenly my great night, my dream come true, had turned into my worst nightmare. I felt like I was onstage with nothing on and everyone was watching, waiting to see what I was going to do. I didn't dare look Georgie in the face. I'd lied to her, so I knew that she'd be looking at me and hating me.

I turned on my heels and fled.

Chapter Five

Old friend, new friend

I ran straight into the closest ladies' room, found a stall, and locked the door. I felt so humiliated. I was sure that all the people around had heard. That was me. The Discount Diva. Silly little poor girl trying to act like she belonged, when everyone could see that she was wearing someone's giveaways. Stupid, sad, pathetic me. I felt so numb with shock that I couldn't even cry. I could hardly breathe either. It felt like someone had put a rope around my chest and pulled it tight. And then I felt a wave of anger. Zodiac Girl. Freaking Zodiac Girl. It was that stupid lunatic at the Internet café who had caused this mess—with his "go back and you will find what you seek" garbage. If it wasn't for that leaflet and that astrology site and that message and that dress, I wouldn't be the biggest *loser* in history, hiding in a public bathroom while everyone outside gossips about what a pathetic, sad reject I am.

I kicked the stall door. "*Eeeeoooooow!*" I cried as I stubbed my toe on the hard wood. I hopped around in the tiny space. It really hurt, like I'd dipped it in fire.

I have to get out of here without anyone seeing me, I thought. *But how? And where could I go?* I wanted to go someplace and hide. But not home. There was no privacy there. Everyone would want to know how the evening went. I couldn't even hide in my bedroom because I shared it with Andrea, and I could hardly shut her out. *Fairy farts*, I thought. *Freaking fairy farts. There was only one thing for it. I'd have to run away. Take to the road and go somewhere where no one knows me. Maybe to Boston or New York. But I'd have no money. And I'd be hungry and have nowhere to sleep except a park bench under some newspaper. And I'd have no friends. And no Mom or Aunt Pat or Phoebe. And no Midnight or Meatloaf to cuddle up to. I'd even miss Dan and Will and Andrea. I'd fade away until someone would find my poor, starved body underneath a bridge, and they'd bring me back here and bury me, and everyone I know would come to my funeral and cry buckets. Even those horrible girls Chloe and Sonia would come and see what happened and realize that they were to blame, and they'd feel responsible as my coffin was lowered into the grave . . .*

As I was sitting there feeling very sorry for myself, I heard the sound of ringing. It was coming from my bag. I looked inside. It was my new cell phone. *But I haven't given anyone the number yet*, I thought. *I don't even know it myself!*

Tentatively, I answered the call.

"Tori, it's Nessa. Where are you?" said a voice at the other end.

Oh, please don't let her have seen what happened too, I thought. "Nowhere," I said.

"Nowhere. Now that's smart," said Nessa. "I've never been there myself. What's it like?"

I almost laughed, but then I remembered that my life was over and I was miserable. "It's . . . okay. I'm not really nowhere."

"You sound upset. What's the matter, darlin'?"

"Nothing."

"Ah, nothing. That always upsets me, too."

This time I did laugh.

"That's better," said Nessa.

"Sorry," I said. "Just, I'm not feeling myself . . ."

"Then who are you feelin'?" asked Nessa.

"No one. I mean, I'm feeling a little weird tonight . . ."

"Ah, that'll be 'cause of the moon. Where the moon is placed in your chart can make everyone feel a little crazy some days. Listen, Tori, I've been lookin' at your chart. Do you know much 'bout astrology?"

"Yes. No. At least I know a little. I know that there are twelve signs and that I'm Taurus and that's the sign of the bull."

"That's right. There are twelve signs. They're called Sun signs. For you as a Taurus, that means the Sun was in the sign of Taurus when you were born. April the twenty-first to May the twenty-first. Anyone born under those dates will be a Taurus. Did you know, though, that there are lots of other celestial bodies that influence your chart?"

"No."

"Well, there are. Ten of them. The Sun, the Moon, Jupiter, Mars, Venus, Saturn, Pluto, Uranus, Mercury, and Neptune."

"Oh, really?" I said, trying to sound interested, although I wondered why on earth she had picked this moment in time to give me a lecture about astrology. "How fascinating."

"Yeah, it is," continued Nessa. "And for you, Saturn and Pluto are squared to your moon at the moment."

"Sounds painful," I joked.

"Right on. No laughin' matter," said Nessa, "'cause what it means is that life is teaching you a serious lesson."

"Oh. What's that, then?"

"Only you can know that, Tori. I'm just here to guide and advise, but Saturn is sometimes known as the taskmaster. In plain English, that means he can be a miserable rascal at times, but you should listen to what he has to say to you. He does talk sense. Pluto is the planet of transformation, and the Moon governs the psyche, feelings, all that kinda stuff. Get those three planets squared up to each other in a chart like they are in yours right now, and it can mean an emotional ride. As a Taurus, I'm your guardian, and I'm takin' special care of you this month, so call me from your new phone if you need or want to ask anythin'. Think of me as a new friend. Okay?"

"Um. Okay," I said, although I couldn't help think, *How weird is this? What is she talking about? In fact, maybe I shouldn't be talking to her at all. Mom always told us not to talk to strangers, and I don't really know anything about her. She may be beautiful, but that doesn't mean she's not bananarama, and come to think of it . . . how did she get my phone number?*

"Um, Nessa, how did you know this number?"

"Because you're a Zodiac Girl this month, right? All Zodiac Girls get a phone like that—well, similar, anyway. We try to make them in the color that's right for your birth sign. The phone came from me. It's so you can get in touch with me, your guardian, or any of the other planets, for that matter. We've all got your new number."

"We?" I asked. I was starting to feel uncomfortable. "And who would the *we* be?"

69

"I told you, me and the other planets. Remember?"

"*Other* planets? Okaaaay . . ." I asked as all my alarm bells went off.

"Yes," said Nessa. "I told you that there are nine others. Celestial bodies, that is. You met one of them. The Sun, AKA Sonny Olympus, he's here tonight. He led the auction, remember?"

"Right," I said, although I was thinking, *Wroooong*.

"And then there's Mars, the Moon, Jupiter, Pluto, Saturn, Uranus—you met him, Uri—he runs the Internet café, and Mercury, he's around somewhere too. You'll like him. All the girls do, though I don't think that there will be any major encounters with him this month, at least not from looking at your chart. You might see him in passing, though. We call him Hermie. Anyway, to cut a long story short, we're all here on Earth in human form."

Whoa!!! I thought. *This lady is not only bananarama— she's the whole freaking fruit bowl. Best to humor her and then avoid her like the plague.*

"Oh, yes. Absolutely. Of course. And you are?"

"Nessa, AKA Venus. Venus rules Taurus, which is why I'm your guardian for the month."

Omigod! She thinks she's a planet! Like how severely delusional can you get? I had heard of people thinking that they were Napoleon or Cleopatra or teapots, but I had never heard of anyone thinking that they were

70

a *planet* before, never mind Venus specifically.

"Guardian. Um. Yes. Um . . . That's what your (*fellow lunatic*, I thought) friend Uri said too."

"Right," said Nessa, "but I hope we can be friends too, because friends are important, right? More important than most things. So come out of your hiding place in nowhere land, and don't be afraid. Not everything is as it seems."

"Yes. Course not," I said. "Actually, I'm feeling fine now. Thanks for the talk. Yes. Better be getting along. Um . . . okay. Got to go now. Things to do. People to see."

"Tori, you sound strange. Are you sure you're okay, hon?" asked Nessa.

"Oh, yes. A-OK. No need to worry about me. All better now. Thanks. Goodbye." *And don't forget to take your medication*, I thought as I heard the door to the ladies' room open and close.

"Call me if you need anything."

"Okey-dokey. Will do," I whispered. *Not a chance*, I thought, but I didn't want to upset her or alert her to the fact that I knew she was a few stars short of a constellation. I also wanted to get her off the phone because I didn't want whoever had come into the bathroom to think that I was the crazy one and talking to myself. Luckily, Nessa had finished whatever she had to say for the time being and said,

"Okay, bye," and hung up.

I clicked the phone shut, held my breath, and pulled my feet up from the floor so that whoever it was wouldn't know that I was in there. A moment later, the door opened again, and someone burst in.

"You *total jerks*," said a voice that I recognized as Georgie's. "That was *way* out of line. Way cruel. So my friend bought your dress. So what? It looks great on her. That's what counts."

The knot in my stomach tightened.

"But you have to admit," said a voice that I also recognized as Sonia's, "it was funny wasn't it, Chloe? Her face turned bright red."

"Purple, I'd say." Her friend snickered.

"And you find *that* entertaining?" asked Georgie. "Ruining someone's night? You sad, pathetic sickos. This is supposed to be a charity ball, you know. Where's your spirit of sharing? Huh? Where? I think you two are possibly the meanest people that I have ever met, and I hope something really rotten happens to you."

"Ooh, get a load of her," sneered Sonia.

"Have you ever heard of karma?" Georgie continued. "Probably not, because you're probably both as stupid as you are horrible. Well, *I* know what it is. It means that your actions bring results, and if you are mean to people, it will come back to you. If not in this lifetime, then in the next. You will probably come back as the lowest of the low. As frog spawn."

The girls started laughing. "Frog spawn? Yeah, right."

"Actually, no, not frog spawn, because frogs are nice. No, you'll come back as flies. Flies that eat poop."

I almost started laughing in my hiding place. *Good one, Georgie*, I thought.

"Oh, let's go, Chloe," said Sonia. "I'm bored with this silly little girl."

"Yes, not my first choice of company either," said Chloe.

I heard the door open and shut again and waited to see if they had gone out.

"Good riddance," I heard Georgie say. There was silence, and then she asked, "Tori, is that you in there?"

I held my breath.

"I know you're in there," she said. "I can hear you breathing."

And then I heard some scuffling, and her face appeared at the gap at the bottom of the door. "And I can see you."

"It's not me," I said and then realized that was totally stupid.

We both burst out laughing.

"Idiot," said Georgie. "I can see that it's you."

"I know. I . . . I'm sorry. I'm sorry I lied. I'll do anything to make it up to you. Be your slave for the rest of eternity . . ."

"Oh, for heaven's sake, Tori. Come out of there. I don't care where you got the dress from . . ."

I lowered my feet back down to the floor, got up, unlocked the door, and went out to join her. "Don't you?" I asked. "See, I did lie to you. I did get the dress from a thrift store, and I should have told you the truth, but . . . I thought you'd hate me."

"No way. You're my friend. I understand. Well. Sort of."

"I went to Osbury to look for a dress, and there this was in the thrift store window, and it looked so fab and . . ."

"You don't have to explain, Tori. I got something from a thrift store once too. A Monopoly game. Why not? Just don't lie to me again."

I still felt bad. Ashamed. "I think I should go home now."

Georgie looked appalled. She put one hand on her hip and wagged a finger at me with the other hand. "Tori Taylor, we are at one of the *bestest* parties we've ever been invited to and you want to go home and leave me on my own! No way. Now that *would* upset me. Just now you said that you were sorry and that you wanted to make it up to me for lying. Okay. Here's your chance. Stay."

"But what if *everyone* knows that my dress is secondhand?"

"*Tooori*," said Georgie in an exasperated voice, "the universe does *not* revolve around you. Probably no one even noticed the two ugly sisters having it out with you just now. And, anyway, I bet you anything that most of the people here have rented their outfits, and that's no different to wearing something secondhand, is it?"

"I guess," I said.

"And most of them are more concerned about what *they* look like and having a good time than where some teenage girl got her dress from . . ."

"Suppose."

"So let's go."

She opened the bathroom door for me, tucked her hand through my arm, and shoved me out.

"Who died and made you the boss?" I said, but I squeezed her arm as I said it, and she gave me a big smile back. She was a good friend. I hadn't realized until that night just how good, but here she was sticking up for me and talking me out of my misery. *Phew*, I thought, *maybe I don't have to run away after all. That's a relief.* I so wasn't ready to handle starvation, loneliness, and homelessness.

As we made our way back into the party, I saw that Georgie was right. No one was the slightest bit interested in me or what I was up to. They were all too busy enjoying the fun. Suddenly it didn't matter that my dress was secondhand. I had one of the best friends in the world, and the evening wasn't over yet.

As we made our way down the corridor, I spotted Mr. O. talking to the mayor and then checking his appearance and smoothing his hair down in a mirror.

I nudged Georgie to look.

"Looks like a poseur, don't you think?" she remarked.

"Yeah," I said, "But I bet that he'd be a heartthrob for the older ladies, though, you know?"

"I guess," said Georgie.

"Hold on a sec. I just want to ask him something," I said. *If Mr. O. knows the mayor*, I thought, *and he runs the auction, then he must be on the level. And he might be able to shed some light on whether Nessa is totally nuts or not.*

"Okay, I'll see you in the disco, then?" said Georgie, and she took off in the direction of the dance hall.

"Okay," I called after her and went over to Mr. O. "Excuse me, sir, but . . ."

"Ah, Zodiac Girl," he said. "Call me Sonny. So how goes it in the land of Taurus?"

"Um . . . good, I guess. About this zodiac thing.

I wanted to ask you if you know what it's all about. I mean, where did that phone you gave me come from, and who's that lady you came with?

His face lit up with a dazzling smile. "Ah. Questions, questions," he said, and then he looked me up and down, put his hands on my shoulders, pushed them back, and stepped behind me and thumped me in the middle of my back. "First, girl, look at your posture. Most important thing they teach at acting school. Stand up straight. Come on. Walk tall. Chin up."

He was so commanding that I found myself doing as he asked.

"Good girl," he said and then began doing the look-up-and-down thing again. "Hmmm, yes. Nice dress, Tori. Suits you. Always remember with clothes, it's the way you wear them. One girl can be dressed in designer labels but look like nothing. Another can be dressed in old castoffs and look like a million bucks. All down to posture and confidence."

Oh, no, I thought as I felt my face blush scarlet. *Georgie was wrong. Everyone in the place did know that I was wearing secondhand clothes.* "So you know about my dress?"

"Know what?" he asked.

"That it's secondhand."

"Secondhand? Is it? Marvelous. Good for you.

You've clearly got a good eye. I love a bargain myself. And it's the right dress for you. What does it matter if it's secondhand?"

"I . . . I guess it doesn't . . ."

"See here, Tori, Nessa showed me your chart. Lacking in self-esteem, it said. Needs to value herself more. You need to work on that, which is why I say, Chin up, shoulders back, walk tall."

I laughed. "Bossy, aren't you?"

He looked offended. "I just know what works. So you were asking about the lady I came with?"

"Yes. Is she . . . um . . . ?" I was about to say, "Is she all right in the head?" but then thought he might be offended if she was his date.

"She's a goddess," he said. "A sweetheart. You're lucky to have her as your guardian."

"Guardian. What exactly does that mean?"

"You're a Zodiac Girl, aren't you?"

I nodded. "I guess."

"So, Nessa's yours for a month. Someone-to-turn-to sort of thing. Nothing weird, in case you're worried. Now, would you care to dance?"

"Dance? Me? Oh, I can't . . ."

"No such word as can't . . ." said Mr. O. as he offered me his arm. "Hey, there's the cake maker extraordinaire."

I glanced up and saw Mom about to go into the

ladies' room. She turned and waved when she saw us.

"Mom," I called, "this is Mr. Olympus, Mr. O., I mean Sonny. He's asked me to dance."

Mom blushed. "Oh, I know who he is," she said. "We met earlier. Go ahead, Tori. I'll catch up with Georgie, and we'll come and watch."

Mr. O. took my hand, tucked it through his arm, and we made our way into the dance hall. Once again, I felt people staring, but this time, it was with curiosity and envy. Sonny was easily the best-looking man in the room, even if he was old enough to be my dad. I spotted Sonia and Chloe at the drinks table and gave them a casual wave. Their jaws dropped open. They *so* didn't expect to see me back at the party. Georgie was dancing on the other side of the hall and gave me a thumbs-up when she saw me.

"Okay, young Zodiac Girl," said Sonny as we began to move to the music, "now, shoulders back and dazzle, darling, dazzle."

We fell into a dance routine as if we'd been rehearsing for days. Soon a crowd gathered around us and began to clap. It was like Mr. O. was completely tuned in to me and what move I was going to make next. To the left we stepped, then to the right, in perfect time with one another.

Suddenly, Mr. O. grabbed a rose from a nearby table, held it with his teeth, and began to clap. I got the message, and we went into a spontaneous crazy flamenco.

"Olé, olé, olé, olé," said Mr. O. through his teeth, while I danced around him Spanish style, and the onlookers cheered. When we'd finished, we both burst out laughing, and he gave me a hug.

"Laugh, and the world laughs with you; cry . . ." Mr. O. started to say.

"And you cry alone," I finished for him and gave him a big smile.

"Well done, Zodiac Girl," he said.

An astonished Chloe and Sonia watched from the side, and I could see the envy in their eyes. They probably imagined that I'd be blubbering in a corner somewhere because of them. *Well, I'm not*, I thought. *You can't get rid of me that easily!*

Chapter Six

Miniature people

"That's *so* cool," said Megan after I'd shown her and Hannah my new phone while we were on the bus going to school on Monday morning. Both of them were very impressed, but I still wasn't sure if I was being pursued by the local nut cases. Nessa had sent me a text message before breakfast. "Come to Osbury tonight after school, Nessa ✱✱✱" it said. I noted the star symbols instead of kisses.

Yeah, right, I thought. *Except she might have some creepy-crawly hit man waiting there to kidnap me and sell me to the slave trade in some intergalactic universe deep in space. It happens all the time on TV.*

I didn't really know what to think about the whole zodiac thing, even though Mr. O. had said that Nessa was okay. I wanted to believe him, but, then, he might be the king of the Bongo Beings and she his queen, for all I knew. In the cold light of Sunday morning, I had thought it all over and decided that the whole deal sounded unreal. The entire evening had been extrordinary, and I hadn't exactly been my normal self either. But stars, planets, zodiacs? No, thanks—way too out there for me. But the phone I'd been given was so cute that I couldn't resist taking it to school. Georgie had said that she'd never seen one like it. It would be my chance to show something off for a change. Not that it worked very well as a phone. I had tried typing all of my friends' numbers into it, but it wouldn't save them. And it already had the names of lots of people I didn't know listed in the address book.

Hannah and Meg were dying to hear all about the dance on Saturday. I filled them in on most of it (not the part about the dress, though—I'd had to eat enough humble pie for one week) and told them all about the zodiac thing and how I'd been given the phone and the necklace.

"Wow, I wish I was a Zodiac Girl," said Megan. "It sounds great. Maybe we can try the site at lunchtime in the library and see if I'm one too."

"We can," I said, "but from what I could make out from the guy who runs the Internet café, there is only one each month. And I don't think everyone gets to be a Zodiac Girl."

"So what makes you one?" asked Megan.

"I don't know. I haven't really had a chance to ask much about it. Nessa—she's the lady I told you about who said that she's my guardian—she said something about there being ten celestial bodies all here in human form. But don't you think that sounds crazy? I mean, they might be a bunch of loony petunies, for all I know . . ."

"Nah," said Megan. "I don't think it sounds that weird. It's not like they've asked you to do anything scary like get into a car with them or lured you to a deserted alley. You're not stupid. You know the rules about strangers, and what have they done? They've given you presents. I think they sound like angels or fairies."

I should have known that she'd react like that.

"Let me have another look at the phone," said Hannah.

I passed her the phone, and she and Meg inspected it.

"Wow, it's a camera phone," said Megan, and she held it up to take some pictures. "At least, I think it is . . ."

I hadn't realized that it could take pictures, as I'm not as techno-savvy as her and Hannah.

"Really?" I said. "Let's see."

But Hannah was busy with it. "I can't get it to take pictures, but, oh, look," she said as she pressed a button. "There are already some shots on here. Wow. Who are these people?"

The three of us leaned in so that we could all see.

"And there's a text message waiting for you," said

Megan, who pressed another button and then began to read it. "'Hi. You seemed unsure about everything on Saturday. Here are the guys I told you about. Hope we can be of some help in your month as a Zodiac Girl, Nessa, kiss, kiss,' although she's put stars, not x's. Wow. It's as if she read your mind and knew that you were worried."

"Or maybe she's done this before and coaxed innocent young girls . . ." I began.

"Oh, chill out, Tori," said Hannah. "You watch too many horror movies. Let's take a look at what's on there."

We leaned in again. Megan pressed a button, and a video began to play on the tiny screen. First there was a shot of Nessa with a big smile on her face, standing in what looked like a florist's, as there were huge vases of flowers all around her. She held up her hands, and tiny, pale pink, heart-shaped flowers began to fall like cherry blossoms in the spring.

"Wow. She's really beautiful," said Megan. "Like a fairy princess."

"And look," said Hannah, "the flowers are forming words on the wooden floor in front of her. What are they saying?"

"'Nessa for Venus,'" I read.

"That's so pretty," said Megan, "and, look, here comes another one."

This time, it was Mr. O. who stepped onto the screen. He was dressed in white and was in a field of bright yellow sunflowers.

Megan did a wolf whistle, causing a few people on the bus to turn around and stare at us.

"He's so handsome," said Hannah. "That has to be your Mr. O., right?"

I nodded.

"I think I've seen him in a movie," Hannah continued, "and, look, the sunflower petals are also making words—Sonny for the sun. Wow! Like, how have they done that?"

Megan put her hand on her heart. "Magic." She sighed. "I knew it existed. I just knew it."

"Oh, get real, bozo," I said. "It's *technology*. They can do anything with it these days for business promotions, advertising, or whatever. I mean, look at the *Harry Potter* movies. You don't think that Hagrid the giant is really that size, do you?"

Megan stuck out her tongue at me.

"Don't like the look of this one," said Hannah as the screen dimmed and the city scene was replaced by the interior of a classroom with a blackboard. A very stern-looking man with white hair and a beard sitting at a desk came into view. He peered over his glasses at us and looked like he was very annoyed to be there. He stood up and wrote in squeaky chalk on the blackboard:

"Dr. Cronus. Saturn." Then he stomped off.

"He was at the ball on Saturday," I said. "He spoke to Nessa at one point. In fact, she said something to me about Saturn. Something about him being the one who teaches lessons or something."

Megan shivered. "He looks very strict," she said. "I wouldn't want him as my guardian. What sign does Saturn rule?"

"Don't know," I replied.

"You could ask Nessa afterward," said Megan. "She's bound to know."

The scene on the phone screen was changing again. This time it was to a dark basement with deep, wine-red walls, burgundy velvet curtains, and lit candles in a huge silver candelabra around what looked like a long wooden coffin table.

"Bit spooky," said Hannah.

"I like it," said Megan. "Very goth chic. Omigod, the table's a *coffin*!"

"And it's *opening*!" cried Megan. "I don't like it!"

The coffin was really opening. Someone was in there! And whoever it was was coming out! A man. First he sat up and then stood and stepped out of the coffin. He looked middle-aged, with a dark ponytail, and he was wearing a dark velvet suit and had a burgundy scarf (that matched the curtains) around his neck.

"Matching accessories. Cool," I commented.

Megan had her hands over her eyes. "Can't look, can't look," she said.

"It's a man, Meg," I said as I watched the screen. "He looks okay. Not scary."

He wasn't spooky-looking at all, and soon Megan was watching with Hannah and me again. He had a long face and a big nose, and there was something about him that looked interesting, like you could have a really good conversation with him about all sorts of things. He held out a fisted hand and then opened it to show that there, on his palm, was a caterpillar. The man blew on it, and it became a chrysalis and then a butterfly. He gave a deep bow, and from behind him and the curtains came hundreds of butterflies flying around his head, making a butterfly crown in the air, and then they flew onto the wall to make the words "P. J. Vlasaova. Pluto." Another bow, a flourish of his hand, and he was gone.

"Way to go, Pluto," said Hannah. "Now, *he* was cool."

Back on the screen, the location changed to a seascape. A beach with the waves from the ocean crashing in, leaving lace patterns on the shore as they went out again. A hippie-looking lady danced (like my mom when she's had some wine) into view. Looking at her, I began to wonder if Megan was right and there were such beings as magical creatures. She looked like a water nymph and was dressed in pale blues and greens and had silver-white hair right down her back. As she danced, she wrote on the sand with a big stick. When she'd finished, she danced off along the beach, arms swaying, and on the sand we could read the words: "Selene Luna. Moon child."

Megan's eyes were shining. "If she's not magic, I don't know what is!"

"Yeah," said Hannah. "I *so* have to get one of these phones."

"It's not the phone. They're fairies," Megan enthused. "I'm sure they are. I *knew* they existed. I *knew* it."

"They're not fairies," I said. "They're *celestial beings*."

Hannah and Megan looked at me with surprise.

"I thought you didn't believe what Nessa told you," said Megan. "You said that you thought they were a bunch of nuts. Well, they don't look like nuts to me. They look *wonderful*."

"I . . . I . . . oh . . ." I had surprised myself by saying so definitely that they were celestial beings, not fairies. Maybe I was being brainwashed!

"Is there anyone else on there?" said Megan, and she began counting on her fingers. "How many have we seen? Venus, the Sun . . ."

"Pluto, Saturn, the Moon," Hannah continued. "That's only five. Didn't you say that there were ten?"

I nodded. I had looked them up in Will's encyclopedia last night. "Uranus, Neptune, Jupiter, Mars, and Mercury."

"Let's see, let's see," said Hannah.

At that moment, Megan glanced out the window and then got up quickly. "Oops! Come on. We're here!" she said.

"Omigod!" I exclaimed when I saw where we were. Megan was right. We'd been so immersed in the camera phone that we hadn't noticed that we'd reached the school already.

The bell was ringing loud and clear as we ran for the entrance. *No time to check out the other planet people*, I thought as I stuffed my phone into my backpack. I couldn't wait to see them. Nessa had *so* pulled through with her video, and my suspicion was fading again. The main feeling I had now was one of excitement.

Chapter Seven

More planets!

At break, Hannah and Georgie had to do library duty, so Megan and I headed out into the playground. It was a beautiful, sunny day, so we made our way over to the closest empty bench and rolled up our sleeves, ready to soak up the sun.

"I wonder which birth sign the Sun is the guardian for?" Megan mused as she got an apple out of her bag and started munching on it.

"I'll find out," I said and got out my phone and quickly texted a message to Nessa asking which planet was in charge of which birth sign.

"Do you think maybe that they all hang out in Osbury?" asked Megan as we waited for Nessa to reply.

"Why would they?" I asked.

"Maybe it's like Stonehenge in England, you know, a sort of sacred site. That would make sense, like some places just have a good vibe, and Osbury definitely does. I always like going there, and you said that Nessa told you that the guy with the Internet café is one of the planet people."

"Uri. Yeah, maybe," I said. "Nessa said that they are ten celestial bodies walking around in human form, so I guess they have to hang out somewhere, but . . . how weird does this all sound?"

Megan shrugged again. "I guess it does sound odd, but who really knows who anyone is or where we've come from or what it's really all about? Maybe being a Zodiac Girl is magic."

"For you, maybe, but you know I don't believe in magic the way you do, Meg."

"Yes, you do," she said. "You just have to open your mind to it. Magic doesn't have to be weird. It's all around us. Everywhere. We live with it every day."

"Yeah, right," I said. "Megan's off in la-la land again."

"No, really, Tori," she said, and then she picked a seed from her apple core. "Like this—this is magic."

I patted her on the head. "Megan, my beautiful, crazy friend. Are you on drugs? I hate to upset you, but that there is a seed from an apple."

"Ah, yes. Tiny, isn't it? Looks like nothing, but plant it in the ground, and it will grow and grow—big, bigger than us. It will turn into a tree. A tree that bears fruit and has leaves and flowers." She held up the seed in the air. "And can you see any of that now? No. It's a seed. An insignificant seed, but from it, all that can come. Now *that's* pretty magical, isn't it?"

I hadn't thought about it like that before, but the way she'd put it, I thought, *Wow! Actually, that is magical, and I've never questioned trees or flowers growing from nothing as being weird.*

"I guess. But that's nature. That's different. These tiny people on the phone and Nessa, what's that all really about, oh small-but-wise one? I've been trying to make sense of it all morning. Like, is it some kind of astrology club and they're all members? See, Megan, I was worried that Nessa might be an escaped lunatic. In fact, this morning, I had decided that I didn't want anything to do with them, but then . . . oh, I don't know what to think."

"Don't reject them," said Megan. "I think there's something special about them. There's much more to them than those people who dress up like their favorite characters from a movie or a book or history. More than that. I think that you should trust them and believe Nessa when she says that they're here to help. Give me your phone again, and I'll see if there are any more of them on there."

I gave her the phone, and she pressed whatever she had done earlier on the bus while I looked over her shoulder.

The picture of a deli window filled the screen.

"There's one!" said Megan.

A miniature man with a very large belly appeared

from inside and waved as if he could see us. He had a navy-and-white striped apron on, and he was grinning. He pointed at a display of fabulous-looking cakes in the window, and the screen zoomed in on them for a close-up. One of them was covered in white frosting and had words written in bright blue on it. "Joe for Jupiter," it read.

"Neat," said Megan. "And those cakes look dee-licious."

Suddenly the screen was replaced by shiny blue curtains, which opened to reveal Uri. He was on a stage and wearing the same electric blue jumpsuit that I'd seen him in, but this time he was pedaling a unicycle around in circles and holding a bright blue umbrella in the air. With a flourish of his hand, the air filled with snow. Heavy snow coming down, leaving a blanket on the ground. With one hand, he pointed at the snow, and the words "Uri for Uranus" appeared as if someone had written them with a stick.

"He's the guy who runs the Internet café," I said. "Uri."

"Magic," Megan breathed happily. "I sooo wish I was a Zodiac Girl. I wonder who my guardian would be. Let's see if Nessa has replied to your message."

At that moment, the phone beeped that there was a message.

"You're a Pisces, right?" I asked.

Megan nodded and looked at the message. "Nessa's

replied to your question," she said and then read the message. " 'Aries is ruled by Mars. Taurus by Venus; Gemini by Mercury; Cancer by the Moon; Leo by the Sun; Virgo by Mercury; um . . . Libra by Venus; Scorpio by Pluto; Sagittarius by Jupiter; Capricorn by Saturn; Aquarius by Uranus; and Pisces by Neptune.' So that's me—Neptune would be mine."

"Let's call Nessa. And ask where he is."

Megan quickly dialed the number for Nessa and then handed me the phone.

"Hey, Tori," said Nessa's voice. "Nice to hear from you."

"Um . . . hello. I'm here with my friend Megan, and she's a Pisces, and she wanted to know where and who Neptune is."

"No problem, darlin'. He runs the fish and chips restaurant in Osbury," she said, so I quickly relayed this information on to Megan.

"No way!" she exclaimed. "Ask about Aries. And Mars. Hannah's an Aries."

"And what about Mars?" I asked Nessa.

"Mario Ares. He's in the army. He teaches self-defense and martial arts in Osbury. And before you ask, I run the beauty salon, also in Osbury."

"You mean Pentangle?" I asked.

"Yeah. That's the one."

"It was on the leaflet that you gave me."

"I had to make sure that we met one way or another."

"And will I meet all the planets? Are they all on my phone?"

"Not all of them," she replied. "Zodiac Girls meet some of them during their time. The ones that are predominant in their chart. Okay, got to go. See ya. Call me if you need to."

"Thanks. See ya."

I clicked the phone shut and looked at Megan. "You were right. Osbury. There are lots of them in Osbury."

Megan gave me a smug look. "I know what I'm talking about more than people realize," she said.

I nodded. Maybe she did. Maybe I had dismissed her fairy stories and her theories about magic too easily.

By the time the bell rang, I felt like someone had put a spoon in my brain and given it a good stir. I felt like a whole new world of people and possibilities had been opened up to me, and it was really making me rethink my take on things. Maybe nothing was as it seemed and nobody was who they appeared to be. I was Tori Taylor, but I was also a Zodiac Girl. Nessa ran a beauty salon, but she was also a planet. Ha! Whatever it all meant, magic or madness, I had a feeling that my life was about to get a whole lot better.

Chapter Eight

Help!

"Oh, NOOOO!" I heard Mom cry from the kitchen.

It was Monday evening and I was upstairs working on a secret birthday card for Dan, whose birthday was coming up, as, like me, he is a Taurus. Art is the one thing that I am really good at, and I often make my own cards for friends and family on special occasions. After hearing Mom scream, I raced down the stairs.

"What? What is it?" I asked as a feeling of panic flooded through me. Mom was sitting at the kitchen table with a letter in her hand and a pile of mail in front of her. She looked pale and shocked.

She held up the letter. "I don't believe it," she said.

"What? Mom! Is it Dad? Or Grandma? What's happened?"

Seconds later, Will, Dan, Andrea, Midnight and Meatloaf piled into the kitchen too. In such a small house, nothing goes unnoticed.

"My job," Mom groaned. "I've lost my job."

"But why?" asked Andrea. "Mr. Lowe loves you."

"He's relocating to California," groaned Mom. "We knew it was on the cards, but not so soon. He never said a word about it when I was at work today."

"Coward," said Will. "He should have told you to your face."

"Mr. Lowe's not very good with people," said Mom. "Only with animals. That's why he's such a good vet."

"But won't he sell the clinic?" I asked. "Someone else will take it over, right?"

"Yeah, someone's got to take care of all the local animals," said Will.

"Meow," mewed Meatloaf, as if he was agreeing with Will. Sometimes I swear that cat understands what we say.

Mom nodded. "The letter says that he has sold the clinic, and the new vet is coming with his own full-time staff from his last place. My services are no longer required. No wonder he couldn't tell me to my face. He does say that he's sorry, though."

Dan went over to Mom and put his arm around her. "You can get another job," he said.

"Yes. Another job. Um. Let me make you some tea," said Andrea, and everyone started fussing around, as if tea and toast were going to make everything all right.

Ten minutes later, we sat around munching toast and jam and wondering what to say.

"This may mean that we have to move," said Mom

wearily. "I am sorry, kids, but . . . the rent went up last month, and now with no job . . ."

"But you'll get another job," said Dan again.

"I'll try to, sweetie," said Mom, "but there aren't many around at the moment. Mrs. Nesbitt from next door was only saying last week that she and her sister had been down to the unemployment office, and there was nothing available. Only more cleaning work for the big agencies, and they take most of the proceeds and pay their workers peanuts."

The atmosphere around the table felt as heavy as lumpy oatmeal. This house was tiny for the five of us as it was.

"We'll think of something, Mom," I said. "Something will turn up. When's the rent due?"

"Week from Saturday. I can just about manage that, but after . . ."

"Then we need to put our heads together and come up with a plan," said Andrea.

Cue for Will, Dan, Andrea, and I to put our heads together. Literally. It was a family joke dating back from when we were little. Will started it, and it did make Mom smile to see us all leaning over with the tops of our heads touching like we were in a football huddle. It didn't really help much, though, and if any of us had lice, we'd just passed them on! Ah, the joys of family sharing.

Suddenly I remembered Nessa and her gang of planet people. Who or what they were, I still wasn't sure, but she did say that they were there to help.

"I may be able to do something," I said when we all sat down again.

"Oh, yes? How's that?" asked Mom.

"Um . . . I . . . um, did I tell you about . . . ? No. Um. Probably not. Where to start? Yes. The other day . . . No. Shut up, Tori . . ."

Everyone was staring at me as if I was crazy. I had been about to tell them that I was a Zodiac Girl and had a bunch of aliens at my beck and call but then realized how totally insane that would sound.

"Um . . . just got to go and make a phone call," I said and made a dash for the hall and up the stairs to my room, where I quickly called Nessa on the magic phone.

"Hey, Nessa," I said when she picked up. "I need your help."

"Okay. So what can I do for you?"

"My mom. She's lost her job. Can you get her another one?"

"Get your mom a job?"

"Yeah. You have a salon and Joe has a café and I've met Uri already and he has his Internet place. Don't any of you need sales assistants or something? Mom does cleaning, too."

"Oh, Tori, darlin', it doesn't work like that."

"But I need help, and you said you could help me."

"I will. I will help you, but with the aspects of your chart and how to deal with it. I'm here to help you reach your full potential."

"I'm fine. It's not me who needs help. It's Mom."

"But she's not a Zodiac Girl, Tori," said Nessa. "You are."

"But she is a Zodiac Girl's mom. And whatever affects her affects me, right? We need practical help. Not help with our aspects or potential or whatever. We might lose our house."

"Hold on," said Nessa. "I'm just looking at your chart. Hmm. A couple of encounters with Uri . . ."

"What does that mean?"

"Hard to predict with Uranus. It's the planet of the unexpected. It means that surprises can come like a bolt out of the blue—not that you're going to run into Uri, just his influence. And let's see, what else? Yeah . . . I did tell you that you had some lessons coming up, didn't I?"

I vaguely remembered her saying something like that at the ball. "Yeah."

"So . . . let me see . . . yeah, Tori, it says that you have a tough time coming up. Sorry, doll, but most Zodiac Girls do. That's partly why they get chosen. I mean, what's the point of helping someone whose life is going perfectly? So you . . . looking at what's in front of me, the lesson this month is to somehow pool your resources. You have to learn not to expect miracles to fall from the sky. You have to make it happen."

"Make what happen?"

"Miracles. The solution to your problems. Make it happen."

Make it happen? I thought. *What sort of advice was that? She couldn't be vaguer if she tried.*

"You're a Taurus," said Nessa. "Did you know that all the different signs are either earth, water, air, or fire?"

"No," I said. I had a feeling that she was going to tell me, though.

"Well, they are. All the twelve signs are either fire, air, earth, or water. The fire signs are Sagittarius, Leo, and Aries. The air signs are Aquarius, Libra, and Gemini. The water signs are Pisces, Cancer, and Scorpio, and the earth signs are Capricorn, Virgo, and Taurus."

"So I'm an earth sign. Um . . . that's very nice of you to tell me, Nessa, but what exactly has that got to do with anything?"

"You have to learn to play to your strengths, Tori. See, the earth signs are very good at being practical. Being earth signs, that means that in many respects they are just that—earthed, grounded. They haven't got their heads in the clouds like some signs. So what I'm saying, sweetheart, is that being a Taurus, you will be really good at doing practical things. I'm sure you'll come up with something practical as a solution."

"But like whaaaaaat?" I asked.

"Oh, hold on a minute. Uri has a message for you." She was quiet for a moment, and I could hear a voice in the background. "He says that inspiration will hit you in an unexpected way. Don't worry."

"So you can't get Mom a job?" I asked.

"That's not what I see here," said Nessa.

Useless, I thought. *Totally useless.* "Okay. Thanks," I said, although I was thinking, *Thanks for nothing*.

I clicked off the phone and got up to go downstairs to join the others. I felt disappointed that Nessa hadn't been more helpful, so I gave the hall closet a swift kick with frustration as I went past. The door flew open, and one of Dan's old GI Joe toys fell out in front of me. I promptly tripped over it, went flying onto the carpet, and landed on my stomach. I knelt up to shove the toy back in the closet, but when I opened the door, a hundred things came spilling out on top of me.

"Arrrgghhhhh!" I cried as old clothes, towels, toys, magazines, and games became dislodged from where they had been wedged in. Books came bouncing down from the top shelf, a box of old shoes, and even one of my old Barbie dolls came flying down and landed on my head. "Waaaaoooooo!"

Mom came running up the stairs. "What's going on? Are you okay, Tori?" she asked when she saw me spread-eagled on the carpet, pinned down by a baseball bat, a Monopoly board on my chest, and a "Hula Honey" Barbie sitting on my head.

"Just about," I said as I rubbed my forehead.

Mom glanced up at the now half-empty closet and the contents spilled out all over the carpet. "I guess we *have* been meaning to empty that out for months now," she said with a grin. "Nice of you to remind us."

"Mom, I could have *died* just then."

"Yeah, right," said Mom, but she didn't look very concerned. She was busy looking at the stuff that had fallen out. "We really should get rid of all these things, you know."

I could see that I wasn't going to get any sympathy now that she'd seen that I was all right. All the same, I decided to lay there a second more and groan. And as I did so, it hit me. A flash of inspiration, like a bolt of lightning.

I sat up and removed Barbie's right leg from my left ear. Uri had been right. And so had Nessa. Use your resources, she had said. Inspiration will hit you unexpectedly, he had said. It couldn't be more obvious.

"I've got it, Mom," I said. "I know *exactly* what we can do to raise some extra cash."

Chapter Nine

Making the $$$

I waited until I got downstairs to make my genius announcement. The others were going to be so impressed with my idea. Even *I* was impressed!

"Tori has an idea," said Mom to Andrea, Will, and Dan, who were still in the kitchen stuffing their faces with toast. "Go ahead, Tori."

Mom, Andrea, Will, Dan, Midnight, and Meatloaf looked at me expectantly.

"Flea market," I said.

Their faces dropped, and Will and Dan started chomping again. Midnight and Meatloaf looked enthusiastic, though; in fact, Midnight hopped onto the chair closest to me and rubbed my hand with his nose as if to show me his approval.

"Flea market? Pff," said Will through a mouthful of peanut-buttered toast. "No. What we need is a miracle. We need to win the lottery."

"What sign are you?" I asked.

"Libra. Why?"

"Should have known," I said. "That's an air sign,

you know. Air sign for airhead. Head in the clouds. The chances of winning the lottery are, like, one in a hundred million billion. We can't rely on that. We have to make our miracle happen, and this is something we can do practically."

"Ooh, get a load of her," said Dan.

"And how much do you think you're going to make from a flea market, bozo?" Will asked. "Fifty dollars tops, and how long would that last for?"

"Yeah, and who would want to buy our old stuff? I bet we couldn't even give it away," said Andrea.

"Fifty dollars would be better than nothing," I said. "Let's see you come up with something."

"Actually," said Mom, who had been looking thoughtfully out the window after I'd made my announcement, "it's not a bad idea at all. We have got all that stuff upstairs clogging up the closets. And even more in the attic and in the garage. It wouldn't do any harm to get rid of it. Especially if we are going to have to move. It would give us some more space, at least. And there's a flea market in the big parking lot every Saturday over in Osbury. I've been meaning to check it out for bargains for some time now, but I never thought of going there to sell. Yes, Tori, I think you may be on to something."

"And you could bake some of your cakes, Mom," I said. "People are bound to want a snack while they wander around."

Mom was beginning to look a lot more cheerful. "Yes," she said. "Let's go for it. Dan, get a piece of paper and let's make a list."

That's one down, I thought. *And it's thanks to you, Nessa.*

Plans for the flea market went into top gear. Everybody pulled together. Andrea cleared out lots of her books, Will took out a pile of old CDs, DVDs, and computer games, Dan donated games and toys that he'd outgrown, while Mom and I found piles of old clothes and shoes that we no longer wore.

I texted Nessa once the plan got under way, and every day brought e-mail messages of encouragement from her. They were so beautiful, like works of art. Each one came on a pale blue background; the first had a wreath of white roses around the message; the second had bright yellow sunflowers; the third had a circle of ivy interwoven with white snowdrops; the fourth was framed with a square made up of stars and planets that twinkled on the screen; and the fifth and sixth had a row of tiny bluebirds that chirped around them. *She must be a whiz at technology and knowing how to create these pages,* I thought as I printed them out and stuck them onto my wall.

Each message was simple:

Don't give up.

Quitters never win and winners never quit.

Don't wait for your ship to come in; swim out to it.

Fortune favors the brave.

The longest journey starts with the first step.

Life is what you make of it.

As the week went on, I felt as if the messages were on a loop in my head, playing over and over again. Don't give up. Don't give up. Don't give up. Quitters never win and winners never quit. Quitters never win and winners never quit. Quitters never win and winners never quit . . . I found myself getting fired up with enthusiasm and ideas.

I so wished that I could let the other Crazy Maisies in on my plans, but that would mean admitting how bad our situation was at home, and I wasn't ready for that or their pity. They were off to see another movie on Saturday evening, but once again I'd had to make up an excuse since I didn't have the cash. I'd said that Mom was taking me and the bros to a new restaurant in town. They didn't need to know that it may well be true; we may go to the restaurant—and then help her clean it! And when Georgie asked if I was free earlier in the day to go shopping with her and her mom, I said that I couldn't because we were joining our family at my uncle's country house for a lunch party. And it was true. They were coming to help out at the flea market. We were meeting at a parking lot at the back of Stop 'n' Shop, where lunch would probably be tuna sandwiches, but no one needed details.

As always when I told fibs or half lies, I felt a twinge of guilt. Sometimes I wished that I could tell them the whole story, but I wasn't prepared to lose their friendship. It meant too much to me. Thankfully, there were other people who knew exactly how things were for us since Dad had left. Mom's sisters and their hubbies. And they couldn't have been more helpful.

I called Uncle Kev, and he agreed to drive us there in his van.

Uncle Ernie said that he'd let us have some vegetables and herbs to sell on one section of the stall. His donation was on the condition that I went and helped him with his community garden some nights after school. Remembering what Nessa had said about Tauruses being practical, I agreed to do it. He even said that I could have my own corner of the garden if I wanted. I resolved to make it my new hobby for the future, as I've always liked digging and planting and watching things grow. Since Megan had said that it was magic that stuff grows from nothing, I felt like my eyes had been opened to the natural wonder all around me. I'd always taken it for granted before. I think Uncle Ernie thought I was crazy when I spent ages just staring at the petals of an apple blossom flower like I'd never seen one before.

Aunt Phoebe let us have a bunch of her old china and said that anything she could do to help, she would.

Aunt Pat (who runs a beauty salon) gave us lots of skin and hair product samples.

By the end of the week, our downstairs rooms were filled to the brim with things ready for the sale. Even Dan, Will, and Andrea were getting more enthusiastic.

Uncle Kev arrived at seven in the morning on Saturday, and we all piled into his van. Mom, Uncle Kev, and I were in the front, and the boys and Andrea were wedged in with the garbage bags in the back. Andrea didn't like that at all and complained about the smell of gas all the way there. She's such a grump, although she did look paler than her normal lily-white by the time we arrived.

When we got to the site, we got busy unloading the van.

"So where's the table?" asked Uncle Kev when the last bag had been hauled out of the back.

"What table?" I asked.

"The table to lay all your stuff out on," he said.

Mom and I looked at each other with horror. All around us, professional flea-market people were unfolding picnic tables and setting out their stalls.

In all of the activity, I hadn't thought about where we were going to put anything.

"Haven't got one," I admitted shamefacedly. "What are we going to do?"

Just at that moment, the alluring smell of frying bacon wafted toward us. Uncle Kev sniffed the air. "Yum. Bacon cheeseburgers," he said. "Come on, boys. What we need is a full stomach, and then we'll deal with the problem at hand."

And off they charged without looking back! *Honestly*, I thought, *those boys do nothing else but eat, eat, eat. But bacon cheeseburgers? What a great idea.* I could see that the lady grilling the burgers at the back of the parking lot was doing a roaring business. We had Mom's cakes, but they wouldn't last long. *I should have thought of making sandwiches. Next time, I'll be better prepared.* I made a mental note for my flea market list of essentials: Table. Sandwiches.

"And I'm going to get a cup of hot chocolate," said Mom. "Want one?"

I nodded, and off *she* went, leaving me alone with a pile of black garbage bags and nowhere to put their contents. *I'll have to lay them out on the ground as best I can. Oh, God*, I thought. *This is quickly turning into a disaster.* I looked up at the sky. Clouds were beginning to gather.

"Oh, *nooo*," I said to no one in particular. "*Please*

don't let it rain. No one's going to come if it rains, and Mom's cakes will get all soggy." I turned my face up to the sky again. "Zodiac Girl calling base. Zodiac Girl calling base. Help needed." I looked back at the garbage bags. *Yeah, right,* I thought, *like someone's going to show up out of the blue and make it all okay. Be practical, Tori, that's what Nessa said. There isn't anyone to fix this mess but you!*

At that moment, I saw a dark purple van drive into the lot. It pulled up alongside Uncle Kev's van. Three people got out. One of them looked familiar. He was tall, very pale-looking, with a hooked nose and long hair pulled back in a ponytail. The girl with him was wearing heavy black glasses and had blond hair scraped back in a bun, and the third one was a stocky man with a shaved head. Not someone to mess with, by the look of him. They were all dressed in head-to-toe black and exuded mystery and glamour like they were the crew from a movie set or something. *The tall man is one of Nessa's alien friends from the phone video, the goth man, I'm sure of it,* I thought as he came over.

"P. J.'s ze name, transformation's ze game," he said and gave a low bow. "Nessa sent me for ze Zodiac Girl. Zese are my two assistants, Natalka and Oleksandra." He spoke in a foreign accent that I couldn't place. It was European, but I wasn't sure from which country. He snapped his fingers, and the girl and man who had accompanied him opened the back of the van and pulled out a folded table and a gazebo.

"For ze putting on of your sales items things," said P. J.

"Wow, thanks," I said.

P. J. nodded, and the three of them seemed to go into fast motion, like a DVD on fast forward. Ten minutes later, they had not only set up a table to put our stuff on, but also assembled a small tent with open sides to go over it.

"In case of ze raining," said P. J.

"Fantastic," I said.

"Ve no finish yet," he said, and with another snap of his fingers, his assistants pulled a bag out of the back of their van. It was full of balloons, flowers, and colored streamers that they set about decorating the entrance to the tent with. By the time they'd finished, our stall stood out from all of the others in the lot, and some of the stall holders near us were staring with open mouths.

"It's a flea market," said a sour-faced man who had the stall across from us, "not a department store."

P. J. raised an eyebrow and looked at the man with disdain. "Marketing, my dear sir," he said. "It iz all in ze presentation."

"Thanks so much," I said. "You saved my day."

"You're velcome," said P. J. "Nessa, she like everything to be beautiful. Iz nice to 'ave her as your guardian, yes? Tauruses be very luckiest. Nessa knows about making things look good." And then with a last bow, he, Natalka, and Oleksandra dived back into the van and drove off.

Mom, Dan, Andrea, Will, and Uncle Kev could hardly believe their eyes when they got back.

"What happened?" asked Will. He checked his watch. "We've only been gone around ten minutes. How . . . ?"

"Some friends of mine dropped by to help." I grinned back at him.

"Megan, Hannah, and Georgie?" he asked. "So where are they?"

"No, not them," I said. "Other friends."

"From school?" asked Mom.

"Um . . . not exactly. Um, new friends."

Mom looked puzzled. "New friends? So where have they gone? I'd like to meet them. You never told me that you'd organized this."

How can I possibly explain? I wondered. Mom was very particular about meeting the people who I hung out with.

"They had to go. Um. They're um . . . they're . . ."

"How much for the jigsaw puzzle?" interrupted a lady behind us. She was holding up a box from the table and looking directly at Mom. "Are all the pieces in there?"

"Oh, yes, it's all complete," Mom replied.

Saved for the time being, I thought as Mom turned away and got busy serving our first customer. After the jigsaw lady, there was a constant flow of people browsing and buying and trying things on. I found an old pack of crayons and paper and quickly made up some colorful price tags so that prospective customers could clearly see what everything cost. As Nessa had done with the messages that she'd sent during the week, I made sure that I made each one of them pretty with either a flower or a leaf or a butterfly or something to make it stand out. A few people commented on them and how attractive they were.

None of us stopped until past noon, by which time we'd sold more than two thirds of our stuff and Mom had forgotten all about asking about my "new" friends. All of Mom's cakes were sold in the first hour, plus all of Uncle Ernie's vegetables, and the sale couldn't have gone better—besides the one awkward moment when I spotted Sonia Marks's younger brother looking through the old CDs. I ducked down under the table before he saw me. I couldn't bear to think of him reporting back to Sonia and Chloe that I'd been seen manning a stall at a flea market. It would have given them the perfect excuse to make fun of me again; in fact, I'd never hear the end of it. Luckily, by the time I emerged from under the table, he'd moved on.

I counted up the takings so far.

"Two hundred and fifty dollars already!" I said when I'd finished.

Mom's face broke into a broad grin. "And still a pile of stuff to sell."

"So that will help with this month's rent, won't it, Mom?" I said.

"More than." She smiled back. "And since it's Dan's birthday next Saturday, I'm going to throw a little party for him with some of the takings, *and* I'm going to give each of you ten dollars."

Ten dollars for me! I thought. *Cool. That means I'll be able to go to the movies with the Crazy Maisies tonight without having to worry about not being able to pay my own way.*

At around one, Mom suggested that Andrea and I take a break, so we set off to wander around the other stalls. Andrea wanted to look at the books and was soon getting out her share of our takings to spend. *Insane*, I thought as I left her sifting through boxes of books on one table. *She gets rid of one pile of stuff and then buys another*. I left her to it and wandered off by myself. All sorts of junk was on sale, and I had a good look around to see who was charging how much for what. I also noticed that there were stalls selling new stuff. Homemade cards, photos, frames made out of flowers, leaves, and twigs, flower arrangements, homemade bath products, as well as a whole variety of cakes and snacks. As I was looking at one stall with lavender pouches on it and thinking, *I could make half the stuff I've seen*, someone tapped my shoulder. I turned to see an old man with a beard standing behind me.

I recognized him immediately. It was Dr. Cronus. Saturn, according to the phone video. He was the one who had written his name on the blackboard. He was dressed in an old-fashioned tweed suit and had a bright red tie with a planet-and-star pattern. *Neat*, I thought as I looked at his tie. *I wonder if all of the planet people wear something like that, like a secret club thing that only zodiac members know.* Nessa had been wearing star earrings at the ball, and I had noticed that Mr. O. had a star-and-planets design on his cufflinks.

"Hi," I said with a grin. "Dr. Cronus, I believe. I'm Tori."

He didn't return my smile. In fact, he looked like he was having a major bad day. "I know who you are," he said.

"So, how's it going?" I asked. I couldn't help but feel a rush of excitement. If he was another one of the planet people, maybe he had another surprise for me, like P. J. coming and helping with the stall.

"How's it going? *How's it going?* What kind of grammar is that? Speak properly, girl," said Dr. Cronus.

"I . . . I meant, you know, how are you? How's it hanging sort of thing," I replied. As the words "how's it hanging" came out of my mouth, I knew that I'd said totally the wrong thing, but there was something about the doctor that made me feel nervous.

Dr. Cronus rolled his eyes.

No need to be so grouchy, I thought.

"So come on, then, girl," he said. "I haven't come here to waste my time. What have you learned so far this afternoon?"

"Learned?" I said. "Nothing. It's a flea market." *In case you haven't noticed*, I thought. "We've sold lots of our stuff already."

"Yes, I went past your stall. You did the price tags, I presume?"

"I did," I said.

"Not a bad effort."

"Thanks."

"And you've had a good look around?"

I nodded.

"Notice anything?"

"Yeah. It seems to be more of a craft fair than people just selling old knickknacks."

"Exactly," said Dr. Cronus. "People using their resources. It's inspiring, isn't it?"

I shrugged. "I guess. There's lots of stuff here that people can buy for Christmas and birthdays. Good gifts."

"*Exactly*," said Dr. Cronus again. "And doesn't that make you think?"

"Think what?"

"Think, Tori! About what *you* could do?"

"Me? But I've done a lot. I got our whole stall organized."

"But it doesn't need to end here," said Dr. Cronus.

I laughed. "Oh, I think it will, sir, I mean, Doctor. We've cleared out all of our closets, and I don't think our relatives could donate any more without ending up with empty houses."

"Look around you, Tori. Look around."

I looked around. I saw the same stalls that I'd looked at for the last half-hour. *Was I missing something?* I asked myself. Dr. Cronus was looking at me as if he expected me to say something. "Yes. Um. Great. Glad the rain held off, but it looks like there might be a shower later." What did he want to hear? As sure as strawberries were red, I didn't know, and his stern stare was making me more nervous than ever.

"So have your friends from school come to help?" asked Dr. Cronus.

"Who? Oh, them? No. Um. Busy." His question caught me off-guard. No way was I going to admit to him that I hadn't told my friends that I was spending my Saturday selling old stuff because basically we couldn't afford our rent and barely could afford food.

"I'd have thought that they'd be here with you," said the doctor. "It would be fun." He spat "fun" like it was a dirty word. *Boy, this guy is way too serious*, I thought. *He's so unlike Nessa, Uri, and Mr. O.*

"Nah." I shrugged. "My friend Georgie went shopping in town with her mom. Megan was going out to lunch with her parents to a new restaurant down on the river, and Hannah's at her pony club."

Dr. Cronus looked thoughtful for a moment. "New restaurant? Pony club, huh?" he said. "Your friends sound well-to-do."

I shrugged. "Kind of. Yeah, they are. Anyway, that's how they usually spend their Saturdays." I was about to add, *Which is why they wouldn't see schlepping out here as "fun"*—but I stopped myself just in time. I didn't want this old geezer probing too much and finding out that I pretended that my Saturdays were as glamorous as theirs. He looked like the type who would give me a long lecture about telling the truth.

"Let them in," he said, as if he had read my mind.

I pretended that I didn't know what he was talking about. "Let who in?"

119

"Your friends. They will understand more than you realize. And no one's life is ever how it seems on the outside."

"Tell me about it!" I sighed.

"Tell *them* about it."

The doctor regarded me for a few moments, and I felt like he could see right into my mind and he knew all that went on in there. It was really spooky, and I felt myself blushing. Then, all of a sudden, he looked away and almost smiled. "So, what next, Zodiac Girl?"

"Next? Dunno."

The half smile faded fast. "Dunno? You mean *don't know*. I *do* wish you'd pronounce things correctly. Either way, that's not going to change things, is it?" he asked and then sighed wearily. "I'll tell you something else about Tauruses, Victoria Taylor. As well as being a sign that is good at being practical, being born under the sign of the bull can also produce the laziest of people. They *love* to sit and do nothing. See nothing. Come on, Tori, *think*. What have all these stalls taught you?"

"I don't know. I really don't. Can't you just tell me?" I asked.

Dr. Cronus sighed again, as if the whole encounter with me was exhausting him. "See? That's you being lazy and not using your brain. Okay. I *suppose* I have to spell it out for you. What's your best subject at school?"

"Art."

Dr. Cronus gestured to the stalls with a sweep of his right arm. "And do you possibly think that some of the people here might have been any good at art at school too?"

"Some of them," I said. "And others, even I could do better than them."

Dr. Cronus nodded. "Yes, even *you* could. You could make most of the things here. The cards. The little paintings. The Christmas gifts. It's all in your chart. You're a very creative girl."

I gazed over at a stall to our right. It was selling handmade cards at an extortionate price. And people were paying it, just for some paper with glitter and seeds sprinkled on it. I could do better. *Is that what he's saying?* I asked myself. *That I should be making these things? I mean, organizing a flea market is one thing. But was he saying that I should be making all sorts of things to sell here? Me?*

"But I'm only thirteen," I said.

Dr. Cronus looked at me as if I had said something funny. "Onwee firteen," he mimicked in a little-girl voice.

"Yes. So it's not *my* responsibility to sort everything out. I'm not the grownup."

"Not the gwownup," he mimicked again.

For a moment I saw red. I didn't like this Dr. Cronus. I only liked the nice, *friendly* planet people. I wanted to sock him.

He raised an eyebrow. "You want to hit me, don't you?"

"No," I lied.

"Yes, you do," he said. "Tauruses may be gentle souls most of the time, but they are the sign of the bull, and we all know that when a bull loses its temper, it can see red, and it's best to get out of the way."

I made myself take a deep breath. "I am *not* going to lose my temper," I said, but I was close to it. I'd thought that he'd understood my predicament and had come to help, but he was making fun of me and trying to make me work! Well, I wasn't going to listen. I didn't have to. Just because I was a Zodiac Girl didn't mean that I had to do what old-timers like him said. *You're not my boss*, I thought.

"I'm going back to the stall now," I said and turned away from him.

He burst out laughing as I walked away.

"Oh, Victoria," he called.

I glanced over my shoulder. "Yes?"

"The other thing about Tauruses . . ."

"Yes?" I asked, but made my face look as uninterested as I could.

"Stubborn," he said and rolled his eyes up to the sky. "Oh, but they can be so stubborn."

Chapter Ten

Inspiration

"Hey, how's it going with the planet people?" asked Hannah when we met up at the movie theater.

"Yeah, how's it going being a Zodiac Girl?" asked Megan.

I rolled my eyes. "Not as much fun as I thought," I said as we stood in line to get tickets. "I met that Saturn guy. Dr. Cronus. He's picked up on the fact that I'm good at art. He was ranting about being practical. I think he wants me to make stuff for craft fairs or something crazy like that. Bizarre, huh?"

"How does he know that you're good at art?" asked Megan.

"Oh . . . from my chart," I said quickly, as I didn't want to say anything about the sale earlier that afternoon. "When I got home this afternoon . . ."

"From your lunch at your uncle's?" asked Megan.

"Um . . . yes, um, that. Anyway, there were a ton of messages about websites to check out. And links to websites. I had a quick look. They were mostly for arty sites selling cards and paintings or sites with details of craft fairs in the area. I think he wants me to make knickknack gift-type things as a hobby or something. Doesn't he know that I'm a student? That I have homework to do? Television to watch? Magazines to read? Nails to paint?"

Georgie laughed. "Yes, it's a hard life, isn't it? Some people don't appreciate just how tough it is for us."

"Maybe he was trying to give you some guidance about what you should do when you grow up," said Hannah.

"Maybe," I agreed. She might be right. Already our teachers had begun to talk about it, and some career counselors had been in to give us lectures on colleges and SATs and stuff. "All I know is that I want to be very, very rich."

Megan and Hannah laughed, but Georgie looked sad. "Being rich isn't everything," she said. "I don't think money makes you happy. I want more than that."

"Like what?" I asked. I couldn't imagine how anybody could be unhappy if they were as loaded as her.

Georgie shrugged. "Dunno. Like friends. Like people around . . ."

She stopped what she was saying and bit her lip. *She's upset about something*, I thought, and I was about to ask her more about it when Megan interrupted, and I decided that maybe this wasn't the best time to ask Georgie what was going on—she looked like she was about to cry.

"Did Dr. Cronus say anything else?" asked Megan.

I shook my head. "Not really." The words "stubborn" and "lazy" rang in my head, but I blocked them out for the hundredth time since he had said them. His words had struck a nerve, and part of me feared that he was right. It wasn't the first time that I'd been called those things, but I didn't like to think that I was like that. "Um . . . do you think that I'm, um . . . lazy?" I asked.

"No more than the rest of us. Why?" asked Megan.

"Just wondered. What about stubborn?"

"Definitely," said Hannah.

Georgie and Megan both nodded in agreement with her. "Yeah," they chorused. "Very stubborn."

"What do you mean? I'm not, am I? Give me an example."

Georgie laughed. "Um . . . how about not coming on the school trip with the rest of us?"

I crossed my arms in front of my stomach. "Oh, that."

"Yes, that," said Megan.

"Ask your planet lady if she thinks you should go," said Hannah. "Bet she agrees with us."

She'd probably tell me to be practical or get miserable old Cronus to tell me to walk there or something just as unhelpful, I thought, but soon realized that was me being stubborn. And I didn't want to be that. *I'll ask the planet people for advice,* I thought. *I'll show them who was stubborn or not.* I had nothing to lose, and I did really want to go to Italy with the others. "Hold on a sec."

"Where are you going?" asked Megan as I headed off toward the bathroom.

"Bathroom," I called back. I wanted some privacy to text Nessa on my zodiac phone and didn't want them looking over my shoulder.

Once in the safety of the stall, I got the phone out of my backpack and typed in my question. "Need $$$ for trip to pasta land. Any ideas?"

A message came back seconds later. "Use your talents."

I texted back. "Busy at school. Don't have time."

A message came back. "Excuses."

I had a feeling that Dr. Cronus was somehow hogging the line. I texted back. "Is there anyone else there besides Saturn?"

This time, there was no reply, but a minute later, my phone rang. It was Nessa. *Phew,* I thought.

"Okay," she said. "I checked over your chart again. There was the encounter with Pluto and Saturn earlier today. How did it go?"

"P. J.'s way cool," I said, "but Dr. Cronus isn't exactly a barrel of laughs, is he?"

Nessa giggled. "Oh, he has his moments, but I did tell you that he's known as the taskmaster of the zodiac. The one who has lessons to teach. Listen to what he has to say, Tori. It's for your own good, and he's on the level, really he is."

"I have enough lessons at school. Isn't there anything else in my chart? Anything nice?"

"Everybody's chart is a mixture," Nessa replied. "But it's what you make of it that makes the difference whether it's nice or not. Sometimes what you resist, persists. But hold on, there is a good aspect to Jupiter comin' up that should be okay."

"That's Joe, isn't it? Jupiter. The one with the deli. Jupiter's the planet of merriment and expansion, isn't it?"

"Right on the money, darlin'," said Nessa.

"So what does that mean? A good aspect to Jupiter?"

"Well, where it's placed in your chart usually means good luck of some sort. It can mean winnings out of the blue or unexpected windfalls."

I punched the air. That was more the kind of thing that I wanted to hear. Better than old Cronus's ideas. "Excellent."

"And I was thinkin' about your Italy trip," said

Nessa. "Why not suggest to one of your teachers that they hold a raffle? With the money raised, maybe it can sponsor one student on the trip."

Ya-ay, I thought. *What a totally cool idea. Nessa is so nice. I am so glad that she's my guardian, and not old killjoy.* I had a feeling that because the idea had come from Nessa and *I* was her Zodiac Girl and Jupiter was jolly and associated with windfalls and stuff like that, I would win if there was a raffle. That was what she was trying to tell me. I just knew it.

"Thanks, Nessa."

"That's what I'm here for, isn't it? And come by and meet Joe sometime," she said. "He runs the deli in Osbury. Bring your mom. They can talk cakes. He always loves to meet a fellow cook."

"Okay, will do." I said. *I might leave out the fact that he's supposedly the planet Jupiter here in human form, though,* I thought. *Mom would think that I had been taking drugs if I told her that.*

As I went out to join the others, my mouth fell open. Who was standing there outside the theater as if she was waiting for someone? Our teacher Miss Creighton! I could hardly believe my eyes. It was clearly meant to be. Part of a plan. Part of a "get Tori to Italy" plan. *Magic*, I thought as I went straight out to her and told her about the raffle idea.

"Excellent idea, Tori," she said. "I'll get it

organized first thing on Monday morning, as there are a couple of places still not taken. What a smart girl you are."

I beamed back at her. *Italy, here I come*, I thought.

Chapter Eleven

Acceptance

I beamed out at the envious faces in front of me. "Thank you so much for this wonderful prize," I said and then smiled modestly. "And I can assure you that I will do my very best to have the most fantastic time ever."

And then everyone would cheer as I got down from the stage with my ticket to Venice in my hand.

That was my fantasy anyway. Soon to become a reality.

True to her promise, Miss Creighton had put the raffle plan into action, and she confided in me that there had been a fantastic response. By Thursday, she said that there was enough in the kitty to send at least one student on the trip. I knew the prize was mine, not only because Nessa had hinted at it, but also on Monday night, a message had come through from old Cronus socks. "Learn acceptance," it said.

I knew exactly what he meant, and so every evening after school, in front of the mirror in my bedroom, I practiced my acceptance speech. I tried a variety of expressions for when Miss Creighton announced that the winning ticket was mine. Surprise. Quiet dignity. Just a smile. Modest but thankful.

"What on earth are you doing?" asked Will on Friday morning. I'd left my bedroom door ajar, and he caught me at it. It was the day of the draw, and I still hadn't decided what expression to go for when I was announced as the winner and called up in front of the school.

"Say someone won something cool," I said. "How do you think someone should look?"

"Someone? Who's someone?"

"Me, idiot. Say I'm someone. *The* someone. Say I won something. How should I look when it's announced?"

Will shrugged. "Dunno. Don't care. Why? What are you expecting to win?"

"A vacation."

"Can I come?"

"No."

"How do you know you've won or that someone's won?"

"Because Jupiter is favorably aspected in my horoscope."

"Oh, *that* garbage," he scoffed. "Astrology's a big sham, you know. Some stupid journalist is paid to make it all up so that suckers like you will read your horoscope in the paper and think that their lives are going to improve."

"That's not true. At least not all of it. The stuff you read in the papers might be made up, but if you have your own personalized birth chart done, then it's actually scientific."

"Yeah, right. How do you know?"

I didn't know, but I wasn't going to tell him that. "I know because my brain is far superior to yours on account of the fact that I am a girl. So, come on. You must have an opinion. Okay. This is me being told that the prize is mine."

I quickly ran through my practiced expressions for him. Surprise. Joy. Dignified acceptance, etc. He burst out laughing.

"Looks like you've eaten something rotten and need to use the bathroom really badly," he said.

I rolled my eyes up to the ceiling. "I don't know why I bothered to ask you."

"Okay, you should do it like those people at the Oscars, I guess. Just don't start babbling like a baby and thanking everyone from your parents to the mailman."

"Tori, can you come here a minute?" Mom called from her bedroom.

I grabbed my backpack and went to see what she wanted. She put a finger up to her lips, beckoned me inside her room, and shut the door.

"What's the big secret?" I asked.

"Dan," she said. "I've put a birthday present aside for him at the Internet café in Osbury. It's a computer game that he's had his eye on for ages." She handed me a $20 bill. "I called yesterday and said that someone would be in to buy the game tonight. I might not finish work until the store is closed, so can you go there after school?"

I nodded. "Sure. I know exactly where the place is."

"Excellent," said Mom. "And we'll have a great time tomorrow, okay? You have invited the Crazy Maisies to the party, haven't you?"

"Um . . . I think they're busy," I said, "but I'll try again."

I hadn't invited them because, as always, I didn't want to take the risk of one of them asking too many questions about when the house would be finished and blowing my cover. What they didn't know about, they wouldn't miss.

Mom gave me the money, and after a last check in the mirror, I set off for school. I couldn't wait. In just over an hour, my place on the school trip would be secure. I had already laid out the clothes that I was going to take, and earlier in the week at school, I had happily joined in with all the talk about the places we'd see and what we were going to wear. I'd wear my Suzie Tsang dress—it would look so cool with some black sunglasses. And I'd buy some red lipstick. I'd seen the models in my magazines wearing it really bright this year. Cherry red was the new red.

The rest of the Crazy Maisies didn't know that my only chance of going was the raffle. They thought it was a done deal and that I'd changed my mind after the movie outing and signed and paid up like they had. It would be okay when they saw me win the prize. I'd just explain that I wanted to support the raffle.

Assembly was the usual boring mix of announcements and readings, and then at last Miss Creighton took the microphone, and the room got quiet. She was carrying a small hat that she put on the podium in front of her.

As she looked out at the expectant faces, I took a deep breath and tried to calm my rising feeling of excitement.

"I know a lot of you have been waiting for this morning, and I'm not going to keep you in suspense much longer, although I would like to thank everyone for the fantastic response we've had. So now . . . the name of the person with the winning ticket."

She put her hand in the hat and pulled out a ticket.

"And that person is . . ." The silence seemed to go on forever. And ever. And *ever*.

I had to hold myself back from heading for the stage.

"Jane Brightman," said Miss Creighton at last.

I almost fell over as one of my feet set off for the stage and the rest of my body held me back. A cheer went up from the other side of the room, and a flushed Jane Brightman went up onto the stage.

I was stunned, and I'm sure that my face registered an expression that I had *not* practiced in the mirror that week. Horror!

"You all right?" asked Georgie. "You looked like you were about to fall over."

I nodded. "Umpf. Felt a little faint . . . Didn't have any breakfast . . ."

My stomach sank, and I felt as if my heart was about to break as my fantasy disappeared before my eyes and became a reality in front of Jane's. Now I knew what Dr. Cronus's message had really meant. Prepare for acceptance. Acceptance that *someone else* had won my freaking prize. Messages from Dr. C. really were a bad omen.

Chapter Twelve

Planet Earth to Tori

The rest of the day at school went by in a blur as my mind went through my options—or lack of them. What was I going to tell the girls now that there was no way that I could go to Italy? I'd have to fake illness or insanity. Or both. Something. Maybe it was for the best. Maybe winning the ticket wouldn't have been enough, anyway. There was still other stuff that I'd have needed for the trip: clothes, makeup, snack money, magazines for the plane. Mom could never have given me the money for all that. If I was realistic, it had all been a dream. That's what I had to accept. Never mind planets in the sky. I had to come down to where I really was. Planet Earth to Tori. I was a poor girl from a poor family.

Megan, Hannah, and Georgie were very sweet to me all day, like they knew that something was wrong but couldn't figure out what. They fell for my "not feeling well" line and shared their candy at break time, and Hannah did my nails at lunch. And Georgie and Megan tried to make me laugh by doing the zombie shuffle dance that I had invented last Christmas. It involved making your eyes cross, letting your mouth get loose like you're going to drool, bending your knees slightly, and then shuffling along slowly in a line. We always ended up on the floor laughing whenever we did it, and seeing Georgie and Meg trying so hard and acting so crazy did make me smile, but underneath it all, their being nice to me only made me feel worse. I didn't deserve friends like them.

Dr. Cronus had clearly foreseen what was going to happen, I thought. *At least he tried to warn me. And maybe he had been trying to help with his suggestions about me making money through my art.*

I played over my conversation with him again to see if I had missed something. And what had Nessa said about Jupiter? Unexpected windfalls. What was that all about?

At lunch break, I checked my phone to see if there were any other messages on there. Anything that would give me a clue as to what to do next.

There were three voice messages.

Two from Nessa. Her first said, "Your moon is in Cancer, Tori. This means an emotional time." *That probably refers to just now in assembly,* I thought. *That was waaaaay emotional.*

The second message said, "It's not over till it's over."

Did that mean there was hope? It wasn't over yet?

I didn't know anymore.

I listened to the third message. It was from Mr. O. "Take a chance," he said.

Take a chance. On what? The raffle was over. I hadn't won, despite my good aspect to Jupiter. I was beginning to think that Will was right. Astrology was for suckers. And I was the sucker of the week.

As the afternoon classes droned on, I played and replayed everything that had happened since I'd been told that I was a Zodiac Girl. Despite everything, I did want it to mean something. Maybe I'd missed what they were trying to tell me.

Take a chance. Take a chance? What did Mr. O. mean by that? And then it hit me. Of course! It wasn't the raffle that I was supposed to win. It never was. That was just to show me that things could happen. Unexpected things. But I had to *make* what I wanted happen.

I could hardly wait for school to be over so that I could get out and put my plan B into operation. Mission Millionaire. I knew *exactly* how I was going to do it.

"Aren't you coming for a snack?" Megan called after me as I charged out of the school gates. "We're going to Starbucks."

"Later," I said. "Got to pick up something for Mom

that's for Dan. Sorry. Urgent."

I raced off toward the bus stop, leaving the girls looking at me with puzzled expressions on their faces. I didn't want to say too much in case they decided to tag along, and I didn't want any witnesses when I put my plan into action.

I took the bus to Osbury and, once there, headed for the closest convenience store. *When this works out, I'll go and meet this Joe Jupiter person*, I thought as I opened the door to the store and went in.

"Yes, young lady," said the man behind the counter.

I counted my money. I had the 20 dollars that Mom had given me for Dan's present and four dollars left over from my flea market money. I took a deep breath. *It's now or never*, I thought. *Take a chance.*

"Yes, young lady?" said the man again.

For a moment, I almost turned on my heels and ran out of the store, but a voice in my head was urging me on. *Take a chance, take a chance, take a chance. I had to be a Zodiac Girl for some reason*, I thought. *So I shouldn't chicken out now. Now is my chance to change my life and my family's lives.*

I handed the money to him. "Twenty-four scratch tickets, please."

The man regarded me with suspicion.

"For my mom," I said.

"How old are you?"

"Sixteen," I lied. "Anyway, the tickets are for my mom."

The man briefly glanced out the window, and I sensed that he was having doubts about selling them to me, but suddenly he sighed. "Feeling lucky, is she?"

"No. I am. Um . . . that's why she sent me."

"Okay. Which ones do you want? Lucky stars or buried treasure?"

I almost burst out laughing. It was *obvious* which one I should pick. "Oh, lucky stars." I grinned back at him.

"Do you want the one for the top prize of fifty thousand or one hundred thousand?"

"One hundred thousand."

He peeled off the tickets and gave them to me. "Tell your mom to remember us if she wins," he said with a wink.

"I'll do that," I said.

Once outside, I scanned for somewhere private where I could go and see how much I had won. I could hardly wait.

At the other end of the town was a church and the town hall, and next to that was the bus stop. *That'll work*, I thought and set off as fast as I could.

The bus stop smelled damp and musty from last night's rain, but I found myself a corner and set about scratching. The amounts you could win varied: $1, $10, $100, $1,000, or $100,000.

I could hardly breathe with excitement as I scratched off the first ticket. One star appeared. I only had to get three stars, and I'd get a prize. I scratched again. A cherry. And a square. Nope, this card wasn't my lucky one.

Never mind. I had 23 more to go. One of them was bound to be a winner. *Maybe even more than one*, I thought as a rush of excitement surged through me.

On to the next.

One star. A square. And a circle.

Next.

Two lemons and a square.

I continued scratching. Triangles. Squares. Circles. Cherries. Lemons, but no more stars–until there was only one scratch ticket left.

"Please, please let this be the one," I prayed. "Please let Jupiter and his aspects work some magic."

I scratched my last ticket. A star. *Another* star. Omigod, this was going to be it. Two stars. I only needed one more. I scratched away the remaining square as my heart beat in my chest. A . . . a circle. A circle? *Nooooooooo*. It *couldn't* be. I stared hard at the ticket. Two stars and a circle. *Maybe I've missed the winning ticket. Been too much in a hurry?* I thought as I went through them again. But no. None of them had the required three stars. I hadn't even won one *single* dollar.

"NOOoooooo," I yelled as I ripped up the tickets and threw them in the trash. Then I kicked the side of the bus stop. Unfortunately, it was just as an old man went past. He gave me a dirty look. "Stupid young vandals," he muttered as he shuffled on.

I felt like crying. *I am not a vandal*, I said to myself. *I really, really am a loser now. And, oh, God, I've gambled away Dan's birthday present money. How am I going to explain that away? Oh, God, oh, God, oh, God.* I felt as if my insides had turned to heavy, solid stone. What was I going to do? I couldn't go home. I couldn't go to my friends. I'd lied to them, too. Sooner or later, they were going to find out that I wasn't going to Italy. And never had been.

I watched the old man amble along the street, still muttering. *What does he know about my life?* I thought. *What does anyone know about my life and what it's like being me and how much I try? Try to have friends when I can't really keep up with them. Try to be cheerful for Mom when really I'm worried about her and the fact that we might have to move. It's very hard being me and keeping up all the pretense.*

And as for being a Zodiac Girl, what a bunch of garbage that is. I was stupid getting those scratch tickets and I was stupid thinking that being a Zodiac Girl might make me special and I was stupid to believe Nessa's insane story that she and the others were actually planets here in human form.

143

I almost laughed out loud when I thought how dumb I had been. Much more dumb than Megan and her fairies.

I suddenly felt very tired. Exhausted. I felt like lying underneath the bench at the bus stop and going to sleep right there. And never waking up. Tears sprang to my eyes and slowly dripped one by one down my cheeks. I didn't even have the energy to cry right. *No one knows about my life and how unhappy I am sometimes*, I thought. *No one. Not Mom. Not Andrea. Not Will. Not Dan, not Megan, not Georgie, not Hannah.*

As I sat there, it was as if a dam burst, and all of the feelings that I'd been holding back came rushing to the surface, and I began to sob. I felt so stupid. Gambling away the only money I had and Mom's, too. Hard-earned cash from the flea market. I so should have known better. *I'm so lonely*, I thought. *I kid myself that I have friends, but they don't know the real me. The poor me. The liar me. They'd hate me if they knew what I was really like. No wonder Dad doesn't want to live with me anymore. I'm despicable.*

When he walked out on us, for a long time I felt like it was my fault. I never told anyone because I didn't want to have it confirmed. But it's what I felt. My fault. Dads don't leave their children. Not without good reasons. And not only did he leave— he went to the other side of the world. And he

hardly ever calls. *He doesn't love me very much, does he?*
I thought.

As I sat there blubbering, I heard my zodiac phone
ring. I let it ring and ring. "I'm not answering you,"
I said to it. "A lot of good being a Zodiac Girl has
been for me. In fact, if it wasn't for you, I wouldn't be
in this stupid mess."

I chucked my phone in the garbage can where I'd
thrown the useless scratch tickets.

Planet Earth to Tori, I heard a voice in my mind say.
*That's where you belong—down on the ground, not up in the
stars. Yes. Planet Earth to loser.*

Chapter Thirteen

All alone

Five o'clock went by.

Six o'clock.

Seven.

I sat at the bus stop and felt as if I couldn't move. Frozen in time. Inside, I felt numb. Empty. Outside, I felt cold. And . . . *hungry*. God, I was hungry.

But I wasn't going home. I wasn't going anywhere. I was going to stay there until moss grew over me and my skin rotted away and my bones turned to sand. *Yuck, what a horrible image*, I thought as a fresh wave of tears welled up inside me.

A few people walked by. A couple of them stared at me but then moved on. The sky turned gray, and it began to drizzle.

As the light started to fade, I looked up at the sky. The rain had passed, leaving a clear night, with the stars beginning to twinkle, and over the horizon was the silver light of a crescent moon. *I wonder what's really out there*, I thought. I felt so small and insignificant sitting there. *More planets, stars, galaxies? More people like me sitting somewhere on another bench at a bus stop up in space in a parallel universe? Sad and lonely, like me?*

I looked down from the sky and saw a lady with long, silver hair coming toward me. She was dressed in a long, sea-green skirt and an aqua top. I recognized her right away. Selene Luna. The Moon. *Oh, noooooo,* I thought. *Well, you can take a hike, lady. I'm finished.* I sooo didn't want anyone to see me in the state I was in. I was sure that I looked like a complete mess with a swollen nose and bloodshot eyes. And I didn't want anyone feeling sorry for me either.

As she reached the bus stop, I was ready to tell her to go away, but she didn't say anything. Not a word. She gave me the briefest nod and then sat down next to me. She sighed, and then, to my great surprise, she started blubbering. Blubbering like she was going for an Olympic gold medal.

I looked around to see if there was anyone who might know her. Might have upset her. But the street was completely deserted. Not a soul in sight.

It stopped my crying, that was for sure. No way could I compete. She was sobbing so hard that a bubble of snot blew out the end of her nose. *Yuck, impressive,* I thought as I fished around in my pocket, found a tissue, and handed it to her. She blew her nose, sighed a heavy sigh, and then turned to look at me at last.

She still didn't say anything.

"I . . . I . . . know how you feel," I said.

That set her off again. This time, she managed two snot bubbles. One out of each nostril.

I'd never seen an adult with nose bubbles before. Only toddlers, and the sight of hers gave me the giggles. I tried my best to hold back, but as always when I know I'm not supposed to laugh, it just makes me want to laugh all the more. I clenched my jaw, I wiggled my shoulders, I breathed out heavily, but I couldn't suppress it, and out came an explosion of laughter.

She turned on me immediately. "What's so funny?"

"Nothing," I said. "Nothing. Really. I'm sorry. Just . . . oh, it's been a crazy day, and here . . . well, here we are sitting at a bus stop, me crying, you crying . . ." I pointed vaguely at her nose.

She followed my pointing finger and went cross-eyed as she focused on the end of her nose. That made me want to laugh even more, but I wasn't sure how she was going to react, so, once again, I tried to hold it in. *Oh, please don't start crying again*, I thought as her face looked like it was about to crumple. But she didn't. She started to laugh too. And that set me off again. Bigtime. We both sat there and had a really good laugh. It felt great.

When we were both laughed and cried out, she got up.

"I'll be off now," she said.

"Okay," I said.

And that set us off *again*. Laughing our heads off like loony petunies.

Then she bent over, pulled my phone out of the trash, handed it to me, and whispered, "Never be afraid of your feelings, Tori Taurus, and never be afraid to let them out and share them. Now go home. Be yourself. Tell the truth. It's all going to be okay."

I nodded. Yeah, right, like I was going to take advice from a nut case (which she clearly was). But maybe I would go home and confess everything. I had nothing left to lose.

After she'd left, I got out a tissue and blew my nose. I took a quick look at my phone to see who had been trying to call earlier. Missed call from Dr. Cronus, it said. *No loss there*, I thought as I stood up and glanced over at the row of stores across from me. I wasn't ready to go home and face the music just yet. I could see Pentangle, the salon that Nessa owned. Maybe I could go and see if she was there, but there were no lights on when I walked over and looked in the window. At that moment, the smell of cooking wafted past my nose. Onions. Garlic. Whatever it was, it smelled delicious and reminded me that I was hungry. The smell was coming from the deli that Nessa had talked about. As I moved across the street, I could see that inside there were several customers digging into steaming plates of pasta at tables covered in red-and-white cloths. Just watching them made my mouth water. It looked cozy and warm in there, but I had no money left to get anything. I'd gambled it all away.

With a rumbling belly, I moved on. The next store was Uri's Internet café, and as I passed by, I felt a stab of guilt. *How could I have spent the money for Dan's present? That really was the lowest of the low.* I'd have to find a way to make it up to him. Offer to do his homework for the next few years. Let him have the TV remote from now until eternity. Sit in the comfy red seat. Make him grilled cheese sandwiches every night. Be his slave. *I'll do anything,* I thought, *as long as he forgives me.*

The store was closed, but in the window were a couple of state-of-the- art TV sets that caught my eye. Both were turned on and were showing what appeared to be a lecture in a hall. The lecture was being given by an elderly man with a beard. It was my old pal. Dr. Cronus. *There's no getting away from him,* I thought as I began to listen to what he had to say.

"And so in life," said Dr. Cronus from the TV,

"one of the major lessons to be learned is that a person must make their own luck."

"Oh, here we go again," I groaned.

"Who are you talking to, dingbat?" asked a familiar voice. I spun around to see Will standing there with Stu, his tall, gangly friend from school.

"The man on TV," I said. "He said that a person must make their own luck. Listen to him droning on." I could hear Dr. Cronus continuing his speech. "Get up and make it happen, blah-blah-blah." Similar stuff to the messages that Nessa had sent me before the flea market.

Stu and Will were looking at me as if I was crazy. Will tapped the store's window. "D'oh, glass. How can you hear what he's saying?" he asked.

"By listening, idiot. Why? Can't you hear?"

Will and Stu both shook their heads, but I could hear Dr. Cronus as clear as if he was standing right next to me.

"Probably because your ears are full of stuffing," I said.

Stu strained to listen, but shook his head. "Nope, still can't hear anything. You can read lips, can't you?"

"No," I said. "I can hear what he's saying. Can you really, *really* not hear him?"

Will shook his head again.

"She's teasing you," said Stu and sloped off down

the sidewalk.

"I'm not," I said.

But Will had gotten bored too and followed his friend. *Maybe they were teasing* me, I thought as they disappeared around a corner, *and they could hear him and are trying to make me think that I'm losing my mind. That's the sort of sad thing that boys like to do for fun.*

Only one way to find out, I decided as a middle-aged lady approached.

"Um, excuse me, but can you hear what that man on the television in that window is saying?" I asked and pointed at the display.

She looked at the window and then back at me as if I was crazy. "No. No, I can't," she said and hurried off like she couldn't get away from me fast enough.

I was about to follow the boys when I heard a noise coming from the window. I turned back to see Dr. Cronus knocking on the television screen. "Hey, you. I haven't finished with you yet! Yes, you, Victoria Taylor."

"You can . . . you can *see* me?" I said.

The miniature Dr. Cronus in the television set nodded. "Yes, I can see you. I tried calling before, but there was no answer. Now, are you taking in what I'm trying to tell you?"

"Yes. No. *What?*" I asked.

"Make it happen," he said. "Use your talents."

I looked up to the sky. It had grown cloudy again. "Yeah, yeah, so you said."

Dr. Cronus looked angry. He reached out of the television screen and turned himself off. As the visual on the TV faded, I heard him call out two words: "Lazy. Stubborn."

"YOU DON'T UNDERSTAND," I yelled back at the store window, causing yet another passerby to look at me as if I was a lunatic.

I may as well go home, I thought and made my way back to the bus stop. As I stood waiting for the bus, I did some serious thinking. Things were going to change. *I* was going to change. I couldn't go on the way that I had been. I was sick of the lying. And I wanted my friends to like me for who I really was. The Discount Diva. Me. Not who I pretended to be.

In the distance, I could see a bus approaching. *Just in time*, I thought as the sky lit up with a flash of lightning, followed moments later by a rumble of thunder.

As I got ready to flag down the bus, to my left I saw a chubby man running toward me. He reached me just before the bus arrived and thrust two small bags into my hands.

"Two gifts to help you on your way," he said in a Greek accent. "A package for your brother from Uri.

The other from me. No charge for either."

"For me? Oh! Thanks."

"You're welcome. You have made good resolutions to be brave."

"But how do you . . . ?"

He tapped the side of his nose, stuck out his hand, and waved down the bus. When it stopped, the door opened, and he ushered me on. A moment later, it began to pour down.

It was only when I was in my seat that I realized who the chubby man was. Joe. Jupiter. I looked to see what was inside the bags. In one was the computer game for Dan, and in the other was the most delicious slice of vanilla cake that I had ever tasted in my life. My unexpected windfall had arrived after all.

Chapter Fourteen
Dan's day

I made three calls when I got home.

Luckily, Mom was still at work when I walked through the front door, and Andrea and Dan were so absorbed in a movie that they hardly registered that I was back or even that I was late.

I quickly went to find the phone in the kitchen and called Hannah, Megan, and Georgie. I invited each of them to Dan's birthday party. ". . . it's a last-minute thing, really. Mom decided to do it as a surprise, which is why I couldn't tell you earlier," I said as I vowed to myself that this was the last lie I was ever going to tell. "And I . . . I have something really important to tell you afterward."

"Sounds serious," teased Georgie.

"It is," I replied.

The next morning was a hive of activity in our house. Will whisked Dan out of the way to get in some early-morning soccer practice, and the rest of us got busy getting everything ready for the party.

Uncle Kev arrived, and Mom went straight out to the mall with him to get supplies. Aunt Pat and Aunt Phoebe came soon after and started baking and preparing food. Uncle Ernie and Cousin David put up the gazebo that we'd used at the flea market. Andrea was in charge of the decorations, and I went from room to room, helping out wherever I could.

By the time it was noon, the house looked festive and bright, and all of our efforts were worth it when Will brought Dan back. His face lit up to see what everyone had done for him, and when he got his presents, he looked like he was going to burst. *This is the best*, I thought. *Seeing people that I love happy*. Inwardly, I thanked Joe for giving me the computer game. I would have hated myself today if Dan hadn't gotten it because of my stupidity.

The guests arrived—more relatives and their kids, Megan, Georgie, Hannah, neighbors, more friends—and the party was soon in full swing. Will and a bunch of his friends dressed up as clowns and put on a hilarious show for the younger kids, and Megan, Hannah, and Georgie looked as if they were enjoying it all as much as the five year olds.

I was so happy that they had come, as I'd thought that they may have had much more glamorous things to do, but all of them had leaped at the chance when I asked them last night. As I watched them enjoying themselves, the thought of what I had to do and say made me catch my breath with fear. Today was the day that I was going to come clean with them. Tell them the whole story, the truth about me and my family. If they ditched me, then so be it; I had no one to blame but myself.

As the afternoon wore on, the food got eaten, people began to get tired, and the grownups all went inside to relax and have coffee while some of the younger ones played tag. Will and his friends went into the living room to watch TV, and Dan and his friends went up to his bedroom to try out the computer game.

That left me with Megan, Hannah, and Georgie at the tables out back. I began to clear away a few things, stack plates, and put the leftover food in a trash bag, but I knew that the moment would come sooner or later.

And it did.

"So what was it that you wanted to talk to us about?" asked Megan.

"Oh . . ." I started. The three of them were all staring at me so earnestly that I almost lost my nerve. "I . . . I . . . I'm not who you think I am," I blustered.

Hannah laughed. "So, who are you?"

"No. I mean, I *am* Tori. Tori Taylor. It's just that . . . well . . . I've . . ." *This is soooooooo difficult,* I thought. *The most difficult thing I have ever done in my whole life.*

"I've . . . Look, I'm just going to come right out and say it, and I hope you won't hate me forever. Okay. Here goes. I'm a liar. And a loser. And . . ."

"No," said Georgie. "Not a loser."

"And *not* a liar," said Megan.

"Yeah. What are you talking about?" asked Hannah. She looked around with a puzzled expression on her face. "Is this some kind of pretend game?"

"No. I wish it was. I *am* a liar. You don't know," I said. I held out my arms and indicated the house. "For starters, my family is poor. My mom's poor. She works three jobs. Or at least did. She was let go from one of them last week. We may have to move. And . . . we're not redecorating." As the truth came tumbling out, I felt my voice wobble as tears threatened to spill over. "We . . . we couldn't afford decorators. And my uncle hasn't got a big house in the country. He lives in a small apartment a few miles away. And I haven't got any of the things that I said I had, and I can't afford designer clothes. I am a Discount Diva. I get my clothes from thrift stores. We get *loads* of stuff from thrift stores. Books, CDs, games. And I can't afford to go to Italy either. Never could. I have *nothing*. Not even a dad. He went to the other side of the world and hardly stays in touch. He even forgot Dan's birthday today . . ." The thought of that made my eyes fill up with the tears that I'd been holding back, and all of the girls reached out, but I crossed my arms. "Don't be nice. I don't deserve it. I am the *worst* friend in the whole world."

Megan ignored what I'd said and stepped forward and gave me a huge hug. "No, you're not."

"Why didn't you tell us all this?" asked Georgie. "We are your friends, after all."

"Because I thought you'd feel sorry for me because I couldn't keep up. And think I was a loser."

Georgie rolled her eyes. "As *if*."

"Yeah, as if," Megan and Hannah chorused.

The three of them stood there staring at me, and then they looked at each other and then back at me.

It was Georgie who spoke first. "Well, I don't care if you're poor," she said.

"Me neither," said Megan. "I don't hang out with you because of where you live or what you wear."

"Me neither," said Hannah. "I just like you."

"Really?" I gulped back the huge sob rising up in my throat. "Bu . . . bu . . . but . . ." I tried to hold it back, but then I remembered what Selene had said last night at the bus stop in the rain. Share your feelings. Out came the sob, and tears spilled down my cheeks. "Hon . . . hon . . . honest?"

The three of them nodded. "Honest."

"And . . . but . . . can you forgive me?"

They nodded again. "For what?" asked Georgie.

"For not being honest with you."

"Forgiven," said Hannah.

"Group hug," said Megan, and the three of them surrounded me and hugged me.

When they released me, Georgie said, "Now that this is all out, I have something to ask you."

My heart sank. *Oh, no*, I thought. *She's going to ask me something embarrassing, and I'm going to have to confess to even more awful things that I've done and said!*

I decided to try and be brave and face the music. "Okay, what is it?" I asked.

Georgie glanced back at the house. "Um . . . well . . . can we . . . that is . . . can I come over here more often?"

"*Here?* Yes. But why? I mean, of course, but . . . I never thought you'd want to. I mean, your house is fab and . . ."

"Empty," said Georgie, and for a moment, she looked sad. "I hate going back there after school. Mom and Dad don't get home until after nine some days, and yes, okay, the housekeeper's there, but it's not the same. That's why I always love coming here. There are people around, and the house looks lived in. And your brothers are fun. At our house, it's so clinical. You can't relax in case you spill a crumb. I think that here a person can be themselves and even act crazy if they feel like it. I looooove it here. I love that your aunts and uncles come over to help out.

I love that you dress up in silly costumes to watch movies. My house is . . ." And then *her* eyes filled up with tears. "Lonely."

"Group hug," I said, and we all hugged again.

When we pulled back, Megan looked at Hannah. "Anything you need to get off your chest, sweetie?" she said with a big smile.

Hannah looked thoughtful for a moment. "I've always been afraid that you guys might drop me because I'm not as pretty as you are."

"No way," I cried. "You are *so* pretty, but more than that, you're fun."

Hannah blushed, and I swear for a moment that she looked tearful too.

"Megan? You okay?" asked Georgie.

"Yeah. I guess. Except . . . okay, seeing as we're all being honest here," she said as she shifted on her feet and looked awkward, "sometimes I think I'm not as . . . well . . . interesting or funny as the rest of you . . ."

"Noooo waaaay," Hannah, Georgie, and I cried, and then we chorused, "Group hug."

We had another group hug, and then Megan said, "Zombie shuffle."

Immediately we lined up, made our eyes cross, our mouths loose, bent our knees, and began to shuffle around the backyard. In seconds, we all had the giggles, and Georgie lost her footing and toppled over. Megan fell down, Hannah tripped over her, and they pulled me down too. We lay on the ground in a pile and laughed our butts off.

Will leaned out the window and yelled, "Any room for boys in there?"

Georgie blushed this time and gave Will a coy look as she got up and smoothed down her skirt. *Ah! I see exactly why she loves it over here*, I thought, but I didn't mind. From what the girls had said, it looked like I wasn't the only one who was worried, and I wasn't the only one with hang-ups that they were afraid to tell anyone about. I made a vow to myself that in the future I'd be more aware of what my friends were going through and not just think about me and my own problems. And I'd be more honest with them about everything.

Later that evening, Aunt Pat called everyone into the living room, and Mom brought in the cake that she'd baked for Dan. She'd made it in the shape of his favorite chair and iced it in bright red frosting.

"Your very own comfy chair," said Mom.

"Cool," he said.

After he'd blown out the candles and then cut the cake, Aunt Phoebe passed slices around to everyone.

"Hey, you know what your mom should do as a job?" asked Georgie as she munched on her piece.

"What?" I asked.

"Party organizer," she said. "My mom pays a fortune for people to come and plan hers, and sometimes I don't think they're that great. Today has been the best ever. Great food, great entertainment. Your mom would be fantastic at it."

"Yeah," said Megan. "And you could design the invitations and stuff."

"Or make cards," said Hannah. "Birthday cards like the ones you make us."

And suddenly I understood what old Cronus face had been talking about. I could see it all in my mind's eye. Taylor's Terrific Times: birthdays, bar mitzvahs . . . You name it, we could cater for it.

"Hey, Mom," I said, "Georgie's got a great idea for how you, that is *we*, could earn some money . . ."

Epilogue

Taylor's Terrific Times was set up in June of that year after a trial run on my birthday in May. We took advantage of the date coming so soon after we'd made the decision to go into business and used the day as a dress rehearsal. It was fantastic, with homemade presents and cards and a fab lunch with a huge chocolate cake. I felt like a real diva for the day and loved every minute of it, and because everything went so amazingly, it made us all feel a lot more confident about offering our services to the public. By the end of August, Mom was booked until Valentine's Day the following year.

We all pitched in on the weekends.

Mom is the managing director and chief cake maker.

I am the creative director (or, as my brothers call me, Miss Bossy Boots). I do all of the table designs, menus, and invitations.

Will and his friends handle the entertainment (or, as I say, dress up in crazy clothes and act stupid).

Uncle Kev is in charge of transportation.

Aunt Pat and Aunt Phoebe help Mom with the catering.

Andrea researches themes and takes the bookings and handles the accounts.

Dan is the prime cake taster.

I never did get to go to Italy with the other Crazy Maisies, but, in the end, I didn't mind. While they were there, they texted me every day and took so many pictures on their digital cameras that I felt like I had been there with them.

Best of all, though, I finally understood what Dr. Cronus and Nessa had been talking about. I learned about acceptance by seeing and appreciating what I had. Not what I didn't have.

And that has made all the difference.

I'm honest about everything now, both with my family and my friends. I even told Mom about how I felt like Dad leaving was my fault. She was so shocked and reassured me that no way was it because of me. She said that they hadn't been getting along for a long, *long* time and that part of the reason that he didn't leave earlier was because of Andrea, Will, Dan, and me. She said that he never was very good at communicating his feelings, and that was part of their problem. When she said that, it made me think how important it is to tell the people who you love that you care about them and let them know about what's going on in your head, both good and bad.

It's funny because, at the beginning of the month, when my time as a Zodiac Girl started happening, I thought that something cosmic or out there was going to happen that would change my life forever. But it's been quieter than that. Nothing extraterrestrial or weird—just a shift in my attitude. Like I'm myself with my friends now. My real self.

I often see the planet guys in Osbury, and we always stop to chat and catch up. Nessa and Uri are my favorites, and they have been really helpful in helping me with a personal project—and that's making a business out of my greeting cards. Nessa gave me all of her top tips about how to make them look original and pretty (like she did with the messages that she sent me). Uri showed me how I can use all the latest technology to incorporate Nessa's ideas and get images from the Internet. I make all sorts of special-occasion cards, and last week, I had a booth at a craft fair. Georgie, Hannah, and Megan helped me man the booth, and we sold every single card. Uri loves them too and ordered a whole pile to sell in his café!

Next year, when there's a school trip, one thing's for sure and that is that I will be going along with the rest of the Crazy Maisies. And I'll have earned my place on the trip with my own money!

My month as a Zodiac Girl is long over, but I'll never forget it. Or them. Meeting them made me realize that life can be extraordinary, and not because someone is born wealthy or has more money than someone else. What makes a life extraordinary is the people in it. Family and friends.

And I've got the best of both.

The Taurus Files
Characteristics, Facts, and Fun

April 21st–May 21st

Calm and considerate, Tauruses make good and loyal friends. But there's another side to this sign. Tauruses like material possessions and beautiful things, and they've often got their eye on some new designer clothes, expensive food, or five-star treatment of one type or another.

Tauruses are very practical, but they can also be stubborn and lazy. Usually chilled out, they don't like arguing, but if they are really pushed, they can explode. So, if you see a storm brewing over a Taurus's head, you should run for cover!

Element:	Earth
Color:	Green, pale blue, purple
Birthstone:	Emerald
Animal:	Bull
Lucky day:	Friday
Planet:	Ruled by Venus

Taurus's best friends are likely to be:
Virgo
Capricorn

Taurus's enemies are likely to be:
Aries
Gemini
Leo

A Taurus's idea of heaven would be:
A glamorous lunch followed by a super shopping spree—all paid for by someone else.

A Taurus would go crazy if:
They had a job where they had to rush the whole time.

Famous Tauruses:
Andre Agassi
Cher
George Clooney
Kirsten Dunst
Jack Nicholson
Uma Thurman
Renée Zellweger

Here's the first chapter of another fantastic
Zodiac Girls story, **Brat Princess**.

Chapter One

Welcome to my world

"No. I am not ready. Do I look like I'm ready?"

I was lying on a sun lounger by the pool at our villa in St. Kitts in the Caribbean, my cell phone in one hand and a chocolate milk shake in the other. Coco was lying on the lounger next to mine, also wearing sunglasses. She's my dog—a pink bichon frisé. (Everyone at my last school had a little dog, but no one had theirs dyed the way I did. I had to do something—all the pooches looked the same, white and cute—but now Coco stands out in a crowd and matches my new nail polish color perfectly.)

I'd just been thinking how utterly cool life was here on this paradise island, when I was suddenly interrupted by a question as to whether I was ready to leave. Anyone with half a brain should have been able to see that I was in no way prepared to board a flight to Europe. Like, what kind of idiot would travel to Paris in a turquoise bikini, even if it is from Prada's new collection and on everyone's must-have list for the season? We used to live in England when I was younger, so I know how cold it can get in that part of the world. Like, Brrrfreezingville.

"Sorry, Miss Hedley-Dent, but . . ." whined Henry. (He's my dad's chauffeur, personal assistant, and handyman, though you'd hardly know it. In his usual garb of Bermuda shorts and Hawaiian shirt and with his shoulder-length blond hair, he looks more like a professional surfer than a servant.)

"What now, Henry?" I was beginning to get annoyed and would have been more snappy if it wasn't for the fact that my friend Tigsy was on hold, waiting for me, on the other end of the phone.

"Just, um . . . the plane has been ready for some time, and the pilot has been waiting for you for more than an hour."

"So? Tell him that he might have to wait another hour because I'm not ready, and I want to catch some more rays before I leave."

"May I at least give him some idea of when you might be ready for takeoff?"

I gave Henry my best withering look. Tigs and I had practiced it for ages in the mirror at school last year before I got expelled. One eyebrow up, nostrils breathing in, and lips tight. Tigsy said that I appeared more constipated than angry when I did the "look," but, whatever, Henry got the message, backed out of the room, and closed the door. He's so pathetic when he does that droning-on thing. Like, schedules . . . airports . . . Like, it's my problem. Not.

At last I could resume my call. I lay back on the lounger, took a sip of my milk shake, and *yuck* . . . I spat it out. It was WARM!

"Shirla. SHIRLA!" I called.

A few minutes later, Shirla, our Caribbean housekeeper, came out of the house. She always does everything soooo slowly. Like it's all one mighty effort. Probably owing to the fact that she weighs around five million pounds. She's like a house on legs. Legs that are made of jelly, since she doesn't so much walk as wobble her way along. I pointed at the glass. "More ice. And a dab more chocolate."

"Ooh, you likes the chocolate. If you not careful, girl, you going to become one big melted chocolate in that sun," she said as she swayed over, took the glass, and then sashayed off toward the kitchen.

"Oh, and can you get Mason to make me some fries before the flight takes off? Those big square ones he does. And bring a little bowl of that yummy sour-cream-and-chive dip to dunk them in. And something for Coco." (Mason's our cook and Shirla's husband. They're an odd couple; he's as skinny as she is large.)

Shirla stopped for a moment. "Uh, I guess I could," she said, "but you ought to eat some greens one of these days, or else them pimples on your chin there are going to be breaking out all over your pretty little face. And don't you go giving that dog no chocolate neither. It ain't right." She tutted to herself and then disappeared inside before I could say anything.

I picked up the phone again.

"Yum. Fries," said Tigsy at the other end. "Think I'll get our maid to make me some. I love fries."

"Sorry, Tigs, guess you heard all that? Like, welcome to my world. Can you believe it? Henry trying to tell me when we have to leave—like, who pays who around here?"

"*Exactement*," said Tigsy. "You have to let them know who's the boss, yeah?"

"Yeah. It's Mommy's fault. She's way too nice with them all. Like a little mouse. She's like, um, pardon me for squeaking. And Dad's never here, so what can we expect? It's left to me to let them know who's in charge, like I haven't got enough to do as it is."

"Totally."

I stared out over the infinity pool and the ocean beyond. It was glistening with a thousand tiny stars in the afternoon sun. "Yeah. Like, sometimes I think that just because I'm only fourteen, they, like, think that they can tell me what to do. But I say, no way. No way."

"Yeah. No way. Um, but Leonora, I'm not being difficult or anything, but one thing I do know is that sometimes when you're traveling, like, having a tantrum can work against you. Like, it's the beginning of December, coming up to Christmas, right?"

"Yeah. Like deck the halls with boughs of holly, blah-de-blah-de-blah, de-blah-de, yawn."

"So everyone's on the move, yeah? Not just us?"

"I guess."

"Well, I know from when Daddy does his own bookings for when we land our little jet that, if you miss your slot, especially at busy times, you don't get another one."

"Oh. *Un problema*, you think? So you're saying what exactly?"

Tigsy laughed at the other end of the phone. "That you'd better get your filthy rich butt off that island in the Caribbean, Leonora Hedley-Dent, and onto the jet, or else we're not going to be able to have our shopping trip in Paris and get back in time for Christmas."

"Like I care about Christmas. Bah, humbug to all that, I say. It's just another excuse for the staff to skip work for the day," I said, but I did get up, slip my feet into my Gucci mules with the kitten heels, and make my way through the open French doors to my bedroom. Coco got up and followed me. She's soooo cute. She walks like she's wearing heels too.

"I know," said Tigsy. "Three weeks to go, and it will all be one big bore, as usual. The fun part will be you being here and the shopping beforehand, although there will be presents on the day. Daddy said that he might get me a new diamond Cartier watch this year. I've put it on my list since I'm getting tired of my Rolex. It's so last season. But really, Lee Lee, I mean, I'm going to be okay for getting to Paris. I'm in Geneva and only have to hop on a train to get there."

"It's cool. I get you. I'll get a move on," I said as I took a couple of candy bars out of a drawer and flung them into a suitcase on the bed. "I'm packing as we speak, but I'm not going to let Henry think that I'm doing it for him."

"No. Course not. But please hurry. I've got no one to play with over here."

"I'll see you soon."

"Excellent. Kissy, kissy. Daddy's booked us the whole top floor at the George the Fifth hotel. I've been there before, when Imelda Parker Knowles had her sixteenth birthday party there during the summer. It's way cool. I think you'll like it."

"Sorreee. Packing. Be there. Bysie-bye."

"Bysie-bye."

I put my phone down by the bed and went to the mirror, spritzed on some of my Goddess perfume, picked up my brush, and brushed through my hair. I was pleased with the way it was looking. The sun had made my new blond highlights even lighter. One day Shirla had seen me before I'd used my hair straighteners. She said that I had fabulous hair. Ha! She has no idea about the work it takes to keep it looking good. Like, I would be mortified if anyone saw me with my hair in its natural state (curly-wurly), but she said that it suited my birth sign, which is Leo—and my hair, which is halfway down my back, is like a tawny lion's mane. Huh. *Like, why exactly would I want to look like a lion for heaven's sake?* I thought as I applied a slick of mascara. Most of them have ratty manes, hardly the honey-and-fudge organic highlights that Daniel Blake, stylist to the stars, runs through mine!

I put in my blue-tinted contacts to cover my boring brown eyes, applied some concealer over my zits, and glanced around to see what else needed to be done. Coco was watching my every move.

"Oh, don't look at me like that, boo-boo," I said. "I'll only be gone a few days."

Coco rolled over on her back and wiggled on the bed. She's so sweet, even if her belly is a different color than the rest of her. (I ran out of dye.)

Mommy and Shirla had done most of my packing, but I threw a few more things in, just in case. All essentials that they'd missed. Lip-gloss. Latest chill-out CD. More candy bars for emergencies. I glanced over at the photo in the silver frame by my bed. *Can't forget to pack that*, I thought. I never went anywhere without it. It was of me and Poppy, my sister. It was taken when I was 12 and she was ten. Oh. Hair straighteners. I threw them in on top. I couldn't believe that they'd forgotten them, although, actually, I could—another example of how nobody around here has a clue about what matters to me. To travel without them would be like losing an arm or a leg; they're that important. It was hard to know what else I'd need, though. Tigsy said that it was unseasonably warm in Europe, but it wouldn't be as hot as it was here in St. Kitts. The only clothes that I'd worn for the last week were bikinis and sarongs. Still. If it got too cold, I could buy some new cashmere sweaters. I'd worn the ones that I got last December at least three times during the winter season, so I was past due for a few new ones.

I pulled my fave pair of skinny jeans out of the closet and began to put them on. Erg. Arff. They were supposed to be tight, but not that tight!

"MOMMY!!!!"

Mommy appeared at the door a few seconds later.

"Yes, darling?"

"My jeans! They've shrunk."

Mommy came in and watched me struggling to get the jeans zipped up.

"Um . . . you don't think, darling, that you could have maybe put on a teeny-weeny bit of weight, do you?"

I could feel a tantrum coming on. I could feel it in the pit of my stomach, bubbling and boiling like a volcano about to erupt—like, it was all right for her; she never put on an ounce of fat, no matter what she ate. She was so lucky, with her straight blond hair and her perfect figure. She didn't look her age either, and people always thought that we were sisters. As if. It soooo wasn't fair that I'd inherited Dad's frumpy genes and his stupid curly hair instead of hers. "Me? Put on weight? These are MY BEST JEANS. I HAD TO WAIT THREE MONTHS ON A LIST FOR THEM TO COME IN TO THE STORE, AND THAT STUPID HOUSEKEEPER HAS SHRUNK THEM IN THE WASH!"

For a split second, I swear that I saw a hint of a smile cross Mommy's face, which made me even madder. She put her hand on my arm. "Now calm down," she said in a soft voice that made me want to hit something. "You're a growing girl . . ."

I brushed away her hand. "Calm DOWN?

Growing GIRL? I CAN'T GROW ANY MORE. I'M ENORMOUS AS IT IS."

Mommy sighed. "You've got a lovely figure, Leonora, and fabulous long legs. You're . . ."

"WHAT DO YOU KNOW? I'M ALREADY A SIZE SIX, AND EVERYONE IN MY CLASS IS A FOUR OR A TWO! And Lottie James is even a size ZERO! I'M AN ELEPHANT! MY WHOLE DAY HAS BEEN RUINED. I HATE YOU. YOU NEVER UNDERSTAND."

I wiggled out of the jeans. They wouldn't zip up, no matter how much I yanked on the zipper. I tossed them onto the bed and then threw myself, face-down, on after them. And then I went for it.

"WaaaaaaARRRRGGHHHHHHHHHHHHHHHHHHHHHHHHHH!"

I thrashed my arms, pummeled my pillows, and threw my legs up and down. And then I felt sick. Yes, I was going to throw up. I could feel it. I sat up. "And now I FEEL SICK."

Mommy looked at me with wide eyes and an expression of terror. Why, oh, why can't she ever say or do the right thing when I feel like this? I'm sure I'm adopted. I can't be her daughter. We're nothing like each other, and she hasn't got a clue what to do with me. My head started to throb. "And now I've got a headache," I wailed. "And I'm fat. And have zits. And it's your FAULT!"

At that moment, there was a gentle knock on the door, and Henry poked his head around. I picked up a pillow and threw it at him.

"GET OUT! GET OUT. ALL OF YOU. OUT. OUT. I HATE YOU ALL."

Henry disappeared mega fast, and Mommy scurried out like a frightened rabbit.

"WahurggghhhhhhhhhHHHH!" I yelled at the ceiling. "No one understands me. Not anyone. I hate everyone. I hate them all. I hate my life. I'm so ugly. And fat. I am sooooooooooooo unhappy."